THE
HOLIDAY
HOME

BOOKS BY DANIEL HURST

The Doctor's Wife

Til Death Do Us Part

The Passenger

The Woman at the Door

He Was a Liar

The Wrong Woman

We Used to Live Here

The Couple at Table Six

We Tell No One

The Accident

What My Family Saw

The Intruder

The Couple in the Cabin

THE
HOLIDAY
HOME

DANIEL HURST

bookouture

Published by Bookouture in 2023

An imprint of Storyfire Ltd.
Carmelite House
50 Victoria Embankment
London EC4Y 0DZ

www.bookouture.com

ISBN: 978-1-80314-943-1
eBook ISBN: 978-1-80314-942-4

PROLOGUE

The silence in this part of the world is deafening, the area around this luxury log cabin in the Scottish Highlands so quiet and still that it's starting to become unnerving. Or maybe it just feels that way because of everything that has happened since I got here.

I move around the cabin to distract myself from the incessant silence and, as I do, a floorboard creaks beneath my left foot, the noise so loud that it startles me. And now I can hear my heartbeat thudding in my chest.

I suspect I can hear the blood pumping around my body too, or at least feel it, but I know that's not a normal thing to be aware of. I'm usually occupied enough to not be thinking about such a thing, but here, it's as if time has stopped and I'm aware of everything.

Like the call of the bird in the trees just outside the cabin, its piercing shriek cutting through the quiet like a hot knife through butter.

Or like the loud snapping of a branch on the forest floor nearby, perhaps caused by a deer. Or could it be a human?

And lastly, the deafening gunshot in the distance, a sound so loud that it causes me to cover my ears and close my eyes.

When I open them again, I immediately rush over to the window and look outside, afraid of what I might see but needing to check, nonetheless. All I can see are the trees surrounding me on all sides. But that gunshot is still ringing in my ears, and I won't forget it easily.

I need to know who pulled the trigger.

And is anybody hurt?

My husband is out there somewhere, and I know this involves him. I also know that by the time I leave this log cabin behind for good, things are never going to be the same again.

That's because too much has already happened since my family has been here. Shocking secrets have been revealed. Precious hearts have been broken. And now that I've heard that gunshot, it means something even more terrible has happened.

Not everybody who came to this holiday house will be leaving it alive.

TWO DAYS EARLIER

ONE

NICOLA

We left England and crossed into Scotland at least three hours ago, but we've still not quite reached our destination yet. Not that I'm complaining.

Not with views like this passing by on the other side of my car window.

Acres of lush, green pine forests surround the skinny stretch of black road as we move along it, and beyond the tops of the trees come the mountains, their peaks protruding up into a dark and moody sky that my husband, Ryan, thinks holds a storm that will unleash plenty of rain at any moment. The drops of water that begin to bounce off the windscreen a few minutes later prove him right, not that I would ever give him such credit verbally because I wouldn't want to encourage him. He's already right, though, because he was the one who predicted that going to Scotland might not be the best place to get some summer sun when I first mentioned this trip to him. I was optimistic and assumed the weather wouldn't be too bad at this time of year, but I'm being proven wrong so far. As the weather worsens and the mountains become obscured by the low clouds, those of us in the car begin to spend less time looking forward to where we are going and a little more time worrying if we're going to make it to the holiday home intact. That is until the man at the wheel speaks and tries to put our minds at ease.

'This is nothing,' Lewis says with a relaxed shrug of the shoulders. 'You should have seen it the last time we came up here. There was snow on the ground and the temperature on the dashboard told me it was minus eight outside. Ain't that right, Kim?'

'Yeah, it was freezing,' my best friend confirms from her position beside her husband in the front passenger seat. 'I'm pretty sure I had icicles coming off my nose at one point.'

'It wasn't that bad,' Lewis chuckles. 'Was it, Cole? You enjoyed our trip up here at Christmas, didn't you?'

I turn to look at the fifteen-year-old boy sitting behind me in the back of this large people carrier, but he doesn't see me because his head is buried in his mobile phone; the only answer he gives to his father's question comes in the form of a barely audible grunt. That's about as much as anyone in this car has got out of Cole since we set off on this trip four hours ago; the typical teenager has made it painfully obvious that he isn't thrilled about the prospect of spending three days in the middle of nowhere with his parents and their friends. But we're a long way from our homes now and there's no turning back, a thought that doesn't terrify me quite as much as it probably terrifies him, because I've been looking forward to this long weekend. Now that it's here, I'm ready to make the most of it.

The invitation from Kim for our family to join hers for three days at their recently purchased luxury holiday house was too good to turn down, particularly because booking my own stay at a similar property and location would have cost me hundreds of pounds that I can't afford to spend at the moment. But Kim told me that we wouldn't have to pay a penny for this trip, nor would we even have to drive because Lewis was going to take care of that. All we had to do was pack our bags and climb into their car, not even needing to book extra days of annual leave because Ryan and I were already off work to look after our daughter, Emily, during her school half-term.

In fact, the only tricky part of the whole thing was me having to convince Ryan that we should accept the offer of a free holiday in Scotland, because while I've never been one to look a gift horse in the mouth, my husband is somewhat more sceptical about getting something for nothing.

'They really don't want us to give them any money?' Ryan had asked me after I'd told him about the plan. 'Not even petrol for the journey?'

'Nope, though we'll make sure to offer, of course. But they're going up there anyway so it's really not a problem for them to take us too. It's so nice of them to ask, isn't it? I think it'll be fun. Besides, it's not as if we've got anything planned to do here that weekend, is it?'

That last part had been an understatement because money has been tight for us recently, and if not for the chance of a free holiday, I have no idea when the three of us would ever get to go away again in the near future. I'd have loved to have spent Emily's half-term doing fun things with her like taking her to see a movie or the animals at the local zoo, particularly because she's eleven now and growing up far faster than I would like, but we just don't have the funds for any leisure activities at this time.

That's because neither Ryan nor I have particularly well-paid jobs. I work as an admin assistant for a carpet factory, which is as glamorous as it sounds, while hubby is in marketing, though not quite the kind that pays the big bucks. Our jobs are okay and have helped give us a home and raise a child, but our wages have certainly not kept up with the recent dizzying rate of inflation that impacts everything from the cost of a loaf of bread to the hot water we use in our home. But the same can't be said for Kim and Lewis, a couple whose most recent financial outlay, other than this monstrous car we're in, was the second property in Scotland that we're all on our way to now.

'You have to see this place,' Kim told me over a cup of tea just a few months ago. 'It's unreal. It's got four bedrooms, a roaring log fire in the lounge area and there's even a hot tub at the back that overlooks a loch.'

'Wow, it sounds amazing,' I'd replied, doing my best not to feel just the slightest bit envious but struggling all the same.

'It's so peaceful up there, not like around here,' Kim had gone on excitedly. 'Oh my gosh, Nicola, I swear it's heaven. The views literally took my breath away the first time I saw them. I had no idea we had such natural beauty right on our doorstep.'

The part about it being right on 'our doorstep' was a slight exaggeration, because from what Kim had told me about the cabin, it was on the outskirts of a village called Glencoe, in a rural part of western Scotland. A quick Google search after my friend had gone had told me that it was a five-hour drive from where we lived in Preston, a city not too far north from Manchester, so it was hardly local, but the distance involved hadn't put me off wanting to go there because my friend had described it so wonderfully.

The bedrooms. The fire. The hot tub. *I had to see it.*

And once I was asked to go, I was only ever going to say yes.

As we have driven deeper into Scotland it has become obvious that my friend wasn't lying about the natural beauty of this part of the world, long ago passing the signs for the built-up cities like Glasgow and Edinburgh as we moved on into the more rural areas. We drove along the banks of Loch Lomond on our way and through the Trossachs National Park, which was spectacular enough for me, but it's proven to be nothing compared to what has been waiting for us just a couple of hours further north of there. Now we're in the Highlands, an area that another internet search told me was 10,000 square miles of nothing but mountains, lochs, cosy cottages, and even a few castles that are owned by the royal family.

If this place is good enough for the kings and queens of the British monarchy, it's certainly good enough for plain old Nicola from Preston.

There I go again, thinking of myself as old, I say to myself as we drive on. *But I guess turning forty next year does that to me.*

I force myself not to dwell on my next birthday, because I'm supposed to be on holiday and it won't help me relax. Besides, it can't be all bad reaching that milestone. Kim and Lewis turned forty earlier this year and they don't seem to be struggling with it, although maybe being rich helps with that. More money equals less grey hair and wrinkles, or at least I imagine it does. With Ryan turning forty just before I do, I guess we're going to find out exactly what it is like to leave our thirties behind and contemplate a whole new part of life, a period of years that are more commonly associated with middle age than they are with youth. *Oh, to be young and energetic again,* I think before looking at both of the children in the car and seeing that Emily is fast asleep while Cole is still staring at his screen like a zombie.

The rain is getting heavier now, and visibility is reducing, but Lewis doesn't seem to be slowing down as we travel on. If anything, he seems to be getting more enthusiastic the closer we get to the cabin.

'They've filmed loads of movies around here,' he says as he navigates the winding roads that have been carved through this mostly unspoilt area. 'Harry Potter films. *Braveheart.* And a Bond movie, the one where Daniel Craig has a big shootout in the old country mansion right at the end.'

'*Skyfall,*' Ryan mumbles then, referencing the title of the film in question, because while he might be weary from the long journey and still a little grumpy that I agreed we would undertake it in the first place, a Bond fan like him won't miss a chance to display his knowledge.

'That's the one!' Lewis cries, drumming the wheel with his hands. 'So yeah, there's been lots of famous faces up here in the past. And who knows, maybe we'll see something else being filmed this weekend.'

It's clear that Lewis is very proud of this area, or at least proud of the fact that he has been able to afford a place in this area, but I don't mind his enthusiasm because it's nice to learn more about the place we are driving into. And Lewis is only too happy to mention a few more local points of interest, like the fact the cabin we are driving to is only a thirty-minute drive from Ben Nevis, the largest mountain in the British Isles.

'We've talked about climbing up it at some point, haven't we?' Lewis says to Kim as he slows down to approach a sharp bend in the road.

'Yeah, but I'm not sure it's for me,' she replies. 'Too much walking. I think I'll leave it to the boys and stay back at the cabin where it's warm.'

We move around the bend before immediately going straight into another one and all the sudden twisting and turning is making me feel a little travel-sick. I focus less on the view outside the car then and more on the digital display of the Sat-Nav that is part of this vehicle's impressive dashboard and see that we are only three miles and six minutes away from our destination now.

By the time the rain ceases, and Lewis indicates to come off the main road to steer us onto a narrow gravel track that seems to head into the middle of yet another enormous forest, I realise we really are in the middle of nowhere. To confirm it, Kim tells me that the village is over two hours' walk away and even the nearest log cabin to them is on the other side of a deep ridge, which pretty much makes it inaccessible from this side of the ravine.

'Pure privacy,' she says as the gravel crunches beneath the car's tyres and the clouds part above us, bathing this wet part of Scotland in some much-needed sunlight. 'Forget about Preston. Welcome to paradise.'

Any thought that my friend's description of this place as paradise might be a little dramatic is instantly dismissed ten minutes later when I lay eyes on the log cabin for the first time. Sure, Kim has shown me photos of it on her phone before, but they have clearly not done it justice.

Paradise?

That's an understatement.

This just might be the most amazing place I have ever seen.

TWO

NICOLA

An ominous rumble of thunder greets us as we all climb out of the car, not allowing us to get too excited about the brief bit of sunshine we're currently basking in. But I'm not thinking about any incoming storms at the moment. That's because I'm too busy being in awe of the beautiful structure that we have just parked in front of.

The cabin is a wonderful mahogany colour, a deep reddish brown that provides a sense of warmth in amongst the green trees and the darkening sky. It's as wide as it is tall with numerous windows around the property, the top of which has been angled into a sharp point, almost like a tepee, though this is no tent. Nor is this anything like camping, because I can see the interior through the glass of the double-door entrance and it looks like a home fit for a president, never mind a couple of families from a working-class part of England.

'Wow,' I say because it's the only word I can offer at this time.

Ryan says nothing but he has walked over to the side of the cabin and is running his hands over the smooth wooden exterior, clearly marvelling as much as I am at the craftsmanship that went into making a place like this.

'Red cedar logs,' Lewis says proudly. 'You can get them around here, but I believe these particular ones were shipped in from North America.'

Kim has never told me exactly how much this place cost them to buy, and I would never dream of asking her, so I assumed it was mid-six-figures. But now that I'm here and learning more about it, I'm wondering if it was more like seven. Then again, I shouldn't be too surprised because their family home back in Preston is monstrous, easily the biggest house on a new-build estate where the starting prices for properties quickly told me that it was not somewhere I should entertain thoughts of living.

But this isn't even their main house. Imagine having a million pounds to spend on a second home, one that only gets visited a few times a year. Incredible. And Emily thinks so too.

'It's so cool!' she cries, shrugging off her sleepiness and running up the steps before pulling on the door handle to try and get in. Her cute brown ponytails jiggle slightly as she tries the door, ponytails that I am happy she still chooses to have, because I'm sure the day is coming when she deems them childish and takes another step closer to growing up.

'Slow down,' I tell her, but Kim tells me not to worry before she takes out a key and unlocks the door, while Lewis says he will get started on bringing the bags in.

I think about telling Ryan to get our luggage too, but I don't want to deprive him of seeing the inside because he's probably just as intrigued as I am, so both of us follow Kim and Emily in.

The first thing I see is a moose's head mounted above the enormous fireplace, its two antlers protruding from its furry face. Kim tells me she wasn't fond of it at first, it was something Lewis chose, but she feels it adds character to the place now she has got used to it. Below that, in front of the fireplace, is a large sheepskin rug and two L-shaped sofas that are connected to make it look like one big one, both draped in furry rugs that add even more warmth to this place that's located in one of the coldest parts of the UK.

The beams of the ceiling are high above my head, just above a balcony that overlooks this luxurious lounge area, and beyond that are the doors to what I presume are the bedrooms and bathrooms. But before I go upstairs and check out the first floor, Kim leads me into the kitchen area, a section of the cabin that, like everywhere else, is carved out of timber, giving it a truly authentic feel. There's no cheap plastic, chipboard or laminate here, just expensive and expertly crafted planks, from the cupboards to the work surfaces and even the front door of the fridge. It's like stepping into a world of wood, but this is nothing like the small shed in my back garden at home. That shed looks like it might blow over every time the wind gets up, but this place looks so sturdy that it could withstand anything. That is until my husband has a thought.

'Wow, you wouldn't want to light a match in here,' he muses. 'All this wood. The place would go up like a bonfire.'

I'm not impressed that he has chosen to try and downplay the magnificence of this place, even if he's doing it in a subtle, jokey way, but Kim doesn't notice or mind and just gives us more information about this cabin.

'Oh, don't worry about that,' she assures him. 'Everything has been coated in fireproof paint.'

'Of course it has,' Ryan mumbles, but fortunately only I hear that.

'This place is amazing,' I say before my husband can try and find fault with it again. 'Honestly, it's unreal. No wonder you guys wanted to buy it. I'm just surprised you haven't sold your main house and moved here full-time!'

'Believe me, I would if I could,' Kim says without skipping a beat. 'But we need to be in England for Lewis's work and Cole's school so, unfortunately, we can only come up here every now and again. But the plan is to retire here. Isn't it, darling?'

Kim turns to Lewis who walks in with two suitcases in his hand.

'Yeah, but that's a long way off yet.'

He's followed by Cole, who has his own luggage, and immediately walks past us all before heading upstairs with it. But Kim doesn't let him go so easily.

'You're in the small bedroom, remember? Don't go taking your usual room! That's for our guests!'

Cole wearily trudges up the stairs without turning back to acknowledge his mother, and I can't help but wonder if I'm getting a sneak peek into what Emily will be like when she reaches his age just four years from now. It's hard to imagine my polite and spritely little girl ignoring me and acting so moody, but it might be a fate that befalls all teenagers, and I'm aware that it wasn't all sunshine and smiles for my parents either when I was fifteen.

'You haven't seen the hot tub yet!' Kim suddenly exclaims and she ushers me, Ryan and Emily to the back of the cabin and through another set of double doors, before we're on a large decking area with a table and chairs arranged in the middle. But it's the large square item covered with a protective coat that demands our attention, and as Kim peels off the coat and reveals what's underneath, Emily claps her hands and squeals.

'Can we go in? Please? I brought my swimming costume!'

My daughter's excited chatter never fails to bring a smile to my face, and I tell her that she can get in the hot tub but only once we have unpacked.

'Oh, don't worry about that. The unpacking can wait,' Kim says breezily. 'You go get yourself ready, Emily, and I'll fire this thing up. It takes about ten minutes to heat up when we haven't been here but, trust me, it's worth the wait once you're in.'

Kim starts twisting a few dials on the side of the hot tub and it suddenly roars to life, the previously still water on the surface beginning to bubble furiously, and it doesn't take long at all for steam to start rising up into the cold air.

'Oh my gosh, is that the loch?' I say as I notice the incredible body of water in the distance and step to the edge of the decking to get a little closer to it.

'Yeah, not bad, right? It's a shame the weather isn't great today, but the forecast looks much better tomorrow. You should see the loch when the sky is blue. The sunlight reflects off the water and it looks almost magical.'

I'm just about to say that it looks magical enough even in these gloomy conditions when a fork of lightning streaks across the sky above the mountains beyond the loch and, when it does, the whole area is momentarily lit up in a yellow hue.

'Wow, that storm's getting close. Maybe we should go in the hot tub later?' I suggest, but Kim is having none of it as she dips a test strip into the bubbling water to check the alkaline levels.

'Don't worry, this decking is completely sheltered. We won't get so much as a raindrop on us. And besides, I've been in here during a storm before and it's quite the show from this vantage point, I can tell you.'

Kim seems happy with the test results and soon declares the hot tub officially open, so I decide to go inside and help Emily get ready. But we'll need her bag first, so Ryan goes out to the car to get our luggage, while Kim offers to show Emily and I to our rooms.

I climb the stairs while drinking in the sight of the incredible lounge and kitchen as I get higher before laying eyes on what will be mine and Ryan's bedroom for the next three nights. A huge double bed is sandwiched in between a couple of bedside tables and the door to the ensuite bathroom is just beside a large wardrobe that's way bigger than the one I keep my clothes in at home. To top it off, the view from the bedroom window features the loch, and I see another fork of lightning as

I look out and admire the picturesque view that I'll be waking up to during my time here.

'This is beautiful. Are you sure we can't give you some money for us staying here?' I ask my friend when I get another pang of guilt about all of this being free.

'Don't be silly. Make yourself at home,' Kim says with a dismissive wave of her hand before turning to my daughter. 'Come on, Emily, let me show you your room. I think you'll like it. You get your own bathroom too.'

I follow Kim and Emily into the bedroom next to mine and watch as Emily dives onto her big bed and waves her arms and legs out at her sides like a giant starfish.

'Thank you!' she cries, clearly enjoying having a bigger bed to sleep in than the one she has at home, before she races into the ensuite bathroom and proudly proclaims that she has her own mirror to get ready in front of too.

Ryan joins us then, our luggage in tow, and Kim leaves us alone while we quickly unpack. As Emily gets changed into her swimming costume, I hang a few of my dresses in the wardrobe, dresses that I wasn't sure I'd wear if it was chilly here, but this place is already warm and cosy inside, and we haven't even got the fire started yet.

I'm just about to ask my husband if he wants to go in the hot tub too when I notice him staring out of the window with a rather melancholy expression on his face.

'What's wrong?' I ask him, joining him by the window and not missing another opportunity to sneak a peek at that loch.

'Nothing. I'm just tired from the drive,' he mumbles, but I get the sense that there's more to it than that.

If I had to guess, I'd say it's not the travel time that has put him off this place. Rather, it's the fact that he knows he could never afford something like this even if he worked every hour of every day for the rest of his life. His role in marketing at a small publishing house is more about a love for books and literature rather than any desire to accumulate wealth. But I'm not with him for his money so that doesn't bother me and it shouldn't bother him either. Then again, men do tend to think about things like that differently, I suppose.

I'm happy with simple things like companionship and a general sense of security, but men like Ryan often need more, like fast cars, big houses and a constant massaging of the ego, so that probably explains why I am loving my experience here while Ryan is probably trying to come up with some get-rich-quick scheme that could see him buy a place like this one day too. But there's no such thing as a get-rich-quick scheme, or at least one that doesn't end in bankruptcy or prison. 'You know, Lewis can only afford this place because he took the risky decision to start his own business during the recession,' I remind my husband.

'Yeah, I know that,' Ryan grumbles, but I think he might be missing my point.

'What I'm saying is that he deserves the success he has had because it wasn't guaranteed, and we shouldn't envy him or his family for it.'

'I don't envy him,' Ryan mutters, but he's not very convincing.

'Let's just enjoy being here,' I suggest to Ryan, trying to snap him out of his malaise. 'It's been so long since we had a break, so try and relax. It's going to be fun, trust me.'

Ryan reluctantly agrees to snap out of his mood and make more of an effort around the others, and as he finishes his unpacking, I smile at the prospect of a fun few days ahead.

If only I'd known then that the best thing we could have done was stop unpacking, leave the cabin and get as far away from here as possible. If so, then I'd have done it. But I didn't. I just looked back out of the window at the loch and smiled and not even another rumble of thunder was enough to warn me that something bad was about to happen in this idyllic place.

THREE

NICOLA

I check myself in the mirror several times before leaving our ensuite bathroom, feeling extremely self-conscious in the bathing suit that I didn't want to pack but that Kim insisted I did so I could enjoy the hot tub along with everybody else. Now that I'm wearing it, I'm wishing I had followed some kind of healthy regimen over the past few weeks so that I looked a little less squishy around the middle.

I'm hardly obese but I'm a long way from my weight in my younger days, and what's not helping is knowing that Kim has a personal trainer that she sees three times a week. I bet she looks incredible in her costume, or maybe she's not even bothered with a costume and just gone for a skimpy bikini. I probably would too if I was paying hundreds of pounds a month to some guy to give me great abs.

I find everybody else downstairs where Emily is already in the hot tub and soon to be joined by Kim, who, as I thought, looks incredible.

And yes, she went for a bikini.

I notice that Ryan's attention has been drawn to the bikini in question as he stands on the other side of the decking with

Lewis, sipping a beer, but he averts his eyes once he realises that I'm here too. Boys will be boys, so I'll forgive him for checking out my friend. But I kind of hope he isn't checking me out as I quickly climb into the hot tub and submerge my rolls of fat beneath the hot water.

It's relaxing, especially once I'm furnished with a glass of wine, but the atmosphere is momentarily disturbed when Cole appears holding his iPad and demanding to know why the internet isn't working.

'It should be,' Kim says as she sits beside me in this tub. 'Maybe you just need to re-enter the password. It's been a while since we were here. It might have dropped off.'

'I've already done that. It's not working.'

'Well, never mind, you'll just have to join us and converse instead of being online all weekend.'

Cole doesn't like the sound of that and asks his dad if he can fix the internet problem. I watch as Lewis gives it a go, but after checking both the iPad and the wireless router in the cabin, he has some bad news.

'There's no signal at all on the router. Maybe the storm knocked it off.'

That might be the correct verdict as it's a storm that is still very much in full force, because the rain is hammering down on the roof of this decking area and it's very dark now even though the sun isn't due to set for another couple of hours. This is not the weather I imagined for our weekend away.

'Well fix it!' Cole pleads, displaying a whole new level to his grumpiness.

'I'm sorry. There's not much I can do if it's the weather causing the issue. We might need somebody to come out and look at it, but it won't be this weekend, so you'll just have to survive without the internet for a little while.'

Cole huffs and puffs before storming back into the cabin as Lewis makes a joke about the youth of today and their dependence on technology. But Ryan doesn't laugh and, as I keep my eyes on him, I see he still doesn't seem to have fully snapped out of his mood. I also see him opening a second beer, barely five minutes after he opened his first one. Only then does he finally get a little chattier and he makes a comment to Lewis about the Cole situation.

'Try and go easy on him. We all remember how hard it was at his age. School work. Friends. Girls. It's not easy being a fifteen-year-old.'

'It's not easy being the parent of a fifteen-year-old either,' Lewis replies glumly. 'You'll find out in four years when Emily gets there.'

'I'm just saying. He's a good kid. Not everything has to be a battle.'

I'm not sure why my husband has suddenly decided to try and impart some parental wisdom but at least he's being talkative, so I'm hopeful he's warming up to the idea of being here now. I get even more confident about that when he joins us in the hot tub, and with Lewis climbing in too that makes all of us, except Cole who is still sulking inside somewhere.

It would be nice if he joined us, if only so Emily has somebody around who is a little closer to her age, but I doubt that's going to happen for the time being at least. Because of that, and not for the first time, I feel a pang of sadness about the fact that I wasn't able to give my daughter a sibling to keep her company as she grew up.

It wasn't for a lack of trying, because Ryan and I were desperate to have another child, especially Ryan who longed for a son he could take to football games and have kickabouts in the back garden with. But it wasn't meant to be. It was hard enough conceiving Emily and there had been a point when even that seemed like it wasn't going to happen, so I'm more than grateful to just have one child. But that doesn't mean there aren't moments when I think about what it would have been like to have given Emily a brother or sister, and one of those moments is right now as I look at her sitting in this tub surrounded by adults. Fortunately, she seems happy enough and as the conversation moves on to Lewis's business, I find myself unwinding more and more beneath the warm bubbles.

'Yeah, things are going well,' the business owner tells us after Ryan had asked for an update.

'I'd guessed that based on you buying this place,' my husband retorts. 'It must have cost you a fortune.'

'We got a good deal on it.'

'Really? How much did you pay?'

'Ryan!'

I'm embarrassed that he would ask such a personal question, because it's none of our business what our friends pay for things. Then again, they're not really Ryan's friends, I suppose, more mine, so maybe he doesn't think of this dynamic the same way as I do. I've been best friends with Kim since we met in sixth form college, that slightly strange stage of education that comes in the two years between school finishing and university starting. We were both seventeen and found ourselves sitting beside one another in an English class, a subject I had rather naively selected to study further because I'd once harboured grand ambitions of becoming a writer. Just like my dream of having a second child, that one didn't come to fruition either. The extra English classes weren't a complete waste of time because I ended up meeting Kim, and the two of us got on so well that we practically became inseparable throughout sixth form and beyond.

The fact that neither of us opted to go to university in the end and stayed in our hometown made it easier to remain a big part of each other's lives, and once we had both found steady employment, we rented a flat together and entered our twenties with a desire to be as irresponsible as we could get away with. That lasted for a couple of years until we both found ourselves in serious relationships, her with Lewis, me with Ryan, and inevitably we had to kiss goodbye to our bachelorette pad and move into separate homes with our respective partners. But our bond has stood the test of time as we became wives, mothers and even as Kim essentially became a millionaire, which could easily have changed her from the skint student she was when we met.

But Kim has never changed because she has never let the money define her. Sure, she likes to show off this log cabin but only in a way that allows us to enjoy it too. Maybe Lewis is a little different. Maybe he does like to show off a little. And therein lies the problem. Ryan doesn't have a bond to Kim like I do so he can't put up with her husband as easily as me. It's not that Lewis is a bad guy, and Ryan doesn't dislike him as such, it's just that the pair of them have never been particularly close, usually just tolerating each other for the sake of their partners' relationship. Then again, it would be impossible for them to be as close as their wives are. Because of that, I always feel like I'm on my guard a little with them to make sure neither one says something that might irritate the other. Like Ryan asking Lewis exactly how much this cabin cost, for instance.

'Sorry, I shouldn't have asked,' Ryan says when he sees me glaring at him, and Kim quickly tells him not to worry about it before changing the subject, asking what time we might like dinner because she brought plenty of ingredients with her to cook up a huge spaghetti bolognaise.

'My favourite!' Emily cries, already eager for food, even though we stopped at a motorway service station on the way up here and she gorged herself on a cheeseburger and chips.

'I'm starving,' Lewis admits. 'And I'm sure Cole is too. He might be in a mood, but he'll always find time to eat.'

'Maybe I'll go and make a start on the food soon then,' Kim suggests, and I'm just about to offer to give her some help when my husband beats me to it.

'Oh, no, I'll be okay, thank you,' Kim tells him with a smile. 'You stay here and enjoy your beer. You're on holiday, remember.'

Ryan tries not to ogle Kim too much as she climbs out of the tub, but he doesn't do a very good job of it, and he only looks elsewhere once my friend's bare skin is wrapped in a towel and heading inside. I'd be lying if I said it didn't hurt me that he seems to be quite clearly checking out my skinnier friend, but I also know that he'd never do anything to hurt me. Like Cole, who is at the mercy of his teenage whims, Ryan is a male at the mercy of his and an attractive woman right in front of him in a bikini is not something I can expect him to completely miss. I'm also determined not to miss a chance to give Ryan and Lewis a little bonding time, so I suggest Emily and I go inside and help Kim with the food while the two men stay in the tub.

They both look a little awkward about that, but by the time I've got myself and my daughter out and dried off, the men are discussing football transfers, and I'm feeling confident that they are warming to each other after not seeing one another for a while and will be fine this weekend after all. All it took was a couple of beers and a few hours. A few more and they'll be getting along even better, which is good because I want this weekend to be fun. If it is, we can hopefully have plenty more just like it. I certainly wouldn't want to say no if Kim invited us all back here again.

Unfortunately, by the time this weekend is over, there will be zero chance of that.

FOUR

RYAN

I know what my wife is thinking. She's thinking that because I've had a couple of beers and have spent the last ten minutes talking about football that means I'm enjoying myself now. But she couldn't be further from the truth, because despite how it might appear I'm still not having fun, or more specifically I'm not having fun in Lewis's company.

Don't get me wrong, I don't hate the guy. He's pretty harmless and I guess his heart is in the right place. He even has his moments when he can make me laugh, and he certainly likes a drink, which helps endear him to me. It's just that being with him for a whole weekend here at his cabin in Scotland, after a five-hour drive to get here, and after enduring numerous comments about how much money he has thanks to his successful business, is not my idea of fun.

I can tolerate him in small measures. The occasional dinner at a restaurant somewhere on a Saturday night or an hour or so of small talk while our wives are catching up over a cup of tea. Those kinds of occasions are manageable. But a whole weekend, miles from home and with no prospect of getting a break from him? It's going to take a lot more than a couple of beers and some football talk to make that my idea of a good time.

But, just as I promised Nicola I would, I'm making an effort and trying my best to get through it. I know this weekend is more about my wife having a good time with her best friend than it is about me, so that's why I'm trying. I really am. The problem is that Lewis is testing my patience at the same time, and while I've managed it so far, I'm not sure that I'll be able to keep a lid on my true feelings for the entirety of this trip.

Lewis and I are just so different. We might have been born in the same town as each other, and we still both reside there now, but that's about where our similarities end. He's very much a practical businessman, interested in the fast-paced world of industry and finance, chasing money and growing his customer base. I, on the other hand, am more creatively minded and choose to focus less of my professional energies on profit margins and share prices and more on getting a sense of satisfaction from my daily work. That's why I chose to work for an independent publishing house in my hometown, where I help to promote the writing of local authors. There aren't big wages on offer there but I love the sense of wellbeing that comes when we see one of our writers succeed, at least regionally anyway. I'm also passionate about sports, which is why I volunteer at my local non-league football club, giving up numerous Saturday afternoons throughout the year to operate the turnstiles or dish out servings of chips and gravy to the hundred or so people who attend the matches. Again, I do that because it makes me feel good and gives something back, not because I'm trying to get rich.

I doubt Lewis has volunteered at anything in his life. He's the kind of guy who wouldn't do something unless there was something tangible in it for him, and that thing would always have to be cold, hard cash. He asked me about the volunteering once but did so in a condescending way, as if he pitied me and felt like I had nothing better to be spending my time on. He's also asked me numerous times about whether I fancy a career change, the implication being that I'm old enough now, with my fair share of personal responsibilities to boot, to consider doing something a little more financially rewarding. None of my friends would ever suggest such a thing, knowing that it's more important for me to be happy than it is to have a job I hate that might pay well, but, then again, Lewis isn't my friend. He's just the guy who is married to my wife's friend.

The things us husbands have to do for our other halves, hey?

I'll give Lewis one thing though. This holiday home is nice. I didn't want to say it but the logs that were used to construct this cabin are truly beautiful. 'Shipped in from North America' I think he said. Urgh, I wish I could have slapped him when he said that. But most of all, I'm annoyed that it looks as though his money was well spent because this place is definitely worth every penny.

I'm well aware that I could never afford something as grand as this for myself and my family to enjoy. While such a thing doesn't tend to bother me on a daily basis, it does grate on me a little now that I'm here because I know Lewis is thinking that I'm only enjoying such a place as this because of him. I don't want to feel as though I'm in his debt, and he isn't charging me any money for staying here this weekend, but I know he is thinking it. He's thinking that I should be grateful to him for allowing me to be here.

I need another beer.

I'm tempted to leave Lewis and go inside to get another cold bottle from the fridge, but I know the women are busy in the kitchen preparing dinner and I'd rather not get in their way. Nicola and Kim are most likely taking this time to catch up on whatever it is that they couldn't talk about with their husbands present in the car journey up here, so I wouldn't want to interrupt them.

I also wouldn't want to draw another icy glare from my wife, if she sees me stealing a glance at Kim in her bikini again either.

I didn't mean to stare at my wife's best friend as she was getting in and out of the hot tub earlier. It's just that she was right in front of me. Where else was I supposed to look? But I think Nicola caught me and now she probably thinks that I was ogling Kim when I actually wasn't. Whatever. It's hardly the biggest problem in the world. There are worse things to have to worry about. Like how I am supposed to make it through this weekend for one.

There's no doubt about it, it's going to be tough.

If the worst thing that comes of it is my wife is mad at me for looking at Kim, then I guess I'll take that.

That's because far worse things could happen.

But best not to dwell on them too much if I can help it.

FIVE

NICOLA

'Dinner is served!'

Kim's triumphant cry is heard all around the spacious cabin, and it doesn't take long for each of its inhabitants to descend on the long table that is now host to all the food that one of the owners of this incredible place has just finished cooking. I was already nearby, as was Emily, after we had spent the last hour giving Kim some assistance in the kitchen. But the males in our party had been conspicuous by their absence, although they are quickly making up for that now.

It doesn't take long for Ryan and Lewis to make their way inside, their topless torsos still wet from the water of the hot tub, but they quickly pull on T-shirts to appear more presentable for the meal ahead. Cole is also soon on the scene, emerging from his bedroom upstairs and plodding down the stairs with a little more of a spring in his step than the last time I saw him. Then again, if there's one thing that can get a teenage boy to cheer up, it's the smell of a delicious meal.

I'm pleased that Cole seems to be in better spirits as he joins us at the table, his smile as he receives a plate from his mother a good sign that he isn't going to be grouchy with his family members the whole time he is here. I'm also relieved to see that Ryan and Lewis seem to be getting along a little better now, the private time they had together in the tub seemingly having helped them converse enough to no longer be awkward in each other's company. But if there's one thing that can get an adult to cheer up a bit, it's alcohol, so, just like for Cole, it seems there has to be outside factors at play in order for them to be in a better mood. Although if all it really takes to keep the males here happy is food and/or alcohol then they've got everything they need because it's quite the spread laid out before us on this table. Everybody starts to tuck in hungrily, our appetites ravenous after a long day of travel and all the excitement and uncertainty that comes with such a thing.

I make sure Emily has a good amount of food on her plate before I worry about my own, and by the time I have all I need in front of me, Ryan is already halfway through his meal and providing most of the entertainment at this table in the form of the various questions he is asking of the others around it.

'This is delicious. What did you put in the sauce? It tastes better than I remember it.' Kim and I accept the compliment before I give our answer, which isn't a particularly complicated one.

'Just some basil. And a little extra salt.'

'This place is really amazing,' Ryan goes on, the words leaving his mouth almost as quickly as the food is entering it. 'Do you think you'd look to buy somewhere else as well as this?' he asks Lewis after that, who replies by saying they have considered getting a holiday home abroad in the past, but it's more practical to have one in the UK because they can visit it much more without all the fuss of airports to take into consideration.

The questions coming from my husband don't stop there, because he then asks Cole how he is getting on at school and whether or not he feels like he is ready for his big exams that are coming up at the end of his next school year.

Coaxed out of his metaphorical shell a little bit by the question, Cole accepts the opportunity to be more involved in the party, answering the question between bites of his food.

'It's going okay,' he admits with his mouth full. 'My mock exams went well, I think.'

'I heard. It sounded like you did well in English. Is that still your favourite subject?'

'Yeah. And drama.'

'Those were my favourite subjects too. Well, those and history. I had a cute teacher.'

Ryan winks at Cole then and the teenager laughs, which is only the second time I've seen the youngster lighten up since we left Preston. The first time also involved my husband, not long after we had all got into the car and started the journey north. Cole had been moaning about his parents not putting the radio on because they wanted to talk instead, before Ryan had asked him about his favourite musician and shown an interest in the answer, which involved some rapper from New York who wrote songs that were apparently banned from the airwaves in several countries.

Despite my husband not having the slightest clue about that particular genre of music, he had engaged with Cole as the teen had passionately told him all about the music he liked to listen to, and it was a rare moment, before Cole had gone back to being grumpy at his parents' choices again. It was also a bitter-sweet reminder of just how good Ryan would have been with a son of his own, and I'd spent the next ten minutes of that car journey daydreaming about my husband with a little boy, before I had to sadly put that fantasy back into the compartmentalised box I always try and keep it in for the sake of not getting too down about things.

'We just need to work on your maths now, don't we?' Lewis says between his own mouthfuls of spaghetti, a comment that soon removes the smile from his son's face. 'Your mock exam results weren't great in that subject, but we're getting you a private tutor, so that should sort it out, shouldn't it?'

Cole goes back to being quiet then and it's clear the reference to what must be his least favourite subject at school has dampened his good mood that had been on show, for a short while at least.

'A private maths tutor?' Ryan repeats. 'Let's hope she's cute, hey, buddy?'

He gives Cole another wink and the teen laughs again.

'Excuse me,' I say, reminding him that joking about other women's looks is not a trait that I appreciate in my husband. But he is only jesting and it's a playful moment, or at least it is until Lewis takes it seriously.

'It's a male tutor, actually, and the point is we're hiring them for Cole to do some work, not mess around,' he tells us, once again wiping the smile off his son's face. 'It's important that you do well in your maths exam because without passing that, you'll struggle in the real world.'

Lewis might have a point about maths being important, although it's debatable how much he'll really need it, if he plans on pursuing more creative subjects, which it sounds like he might want to do based on what he currently enjoys. But rather than leave it there, Ryan chimes in again with another joke.

'Yeah, how on earth are you ever going to cope as an adult if you can't calculate the length of one side of a triangle or explain Pythagoras' theory to a stranger?'

Cole gets the sarcasm, as does everyone else besides Emily, who is still a bit young and still far too occupied by her food to be listening properly anyway. Because Lewis gets it, he makes it clear that he doesn't exactly appreciate it.

'Sounds like you struggled with maths at school there as well, mate,' he says to Ryan. 'That's fair enough, it is the most difficult subject, I suppose.'

The insinuation about the limits of Ryan's brainpower is

clear but I'd like to think that it's just another attempt at a joke, so I brush over it and try and change the subject, complimenting Kim on the fancy utensils we are using for this particular meal. Unfortunately, Ryan retorts before Kim has a chance to reply.

'I'm just saying, it's not exactly the most exciting subject, is it? I didn't know many kids in my class who enjoyed maths.'

'That might be why most of the kids in your class have dead-end jobs now,' Lewis snaps back before smugly sipping from his bottle of beer, and all of a sudden I'm worried the two men are reverting back to their awkward, slightly argumentative ways.

'Not everybody wants to start their own business,' Ryan comes back with. 'Some people work to live, not the other way around.'

The insinuation there is as clear as the last one. Ryan has always felt like Lewis is obsessed with work, which might be partly true, but as I've reminded my husband in those private moments when we have discussed such a thing, Lewis has his own company so it's not quite as simple as him being an employee for somebody else and switching off at 5 p.m. Lewis is on the defensive right away, although his reply is a pretty good one and it shuts my husband up when it comes.

'I'd say this is living, wouldn't you?' Lewis replies, gesturing to the impressive surroundings, as if to show that while he might be heavily focused on his work, he still makes time to enjoy the finer things in life, finer things that Ryan can't afford himself.

I'm just trying to think of something I can say to distract from the current conversation and prevent this from turning into another example of two men vying for attention, when Cole notices his dad swigging his beer and asks if he could have a bottle himself.

'No, not yet, buddy. Still a while to go until you're eighteen,' Lewis reminds him.

'One won't do any harm,' Ryan suggests, but I'm wishing my husband would just shut up now.

'Maybe not, but my dad kept me from drinking until I was of legal age, and I plan to do the same with my son,' Lewis explains.

'Boring,' Cole mumbles and this time it's Ryan who laughs.

Lewis doesn't look like he appreciates that, but fortunately most of us have finished our meals now, so Kim and I quickly stand up and start clearing away some of the empty plates, diffusing the situation before it has the chance to get any further out of hand.

Cole soon disappears back to his bedroom once the food is done with, and Emily goes to change into her pyjamas, leaving just the adults downstairs. Kim quickly volunteers her husband to put the dirty plates in the dishwasher, if only to distract him from restarting his tense conversation with Ryan, and I increase the odds of that plan being successful by suggesting Ryan go upstairs and make sure Emily is okay.

With both men occupied at opposite ends of the cabin, Kim and I feel confident enough to step outside onto the decking and close the sliding doors behind us, before we acknowledge the elephant in the room, which is the tension that exists between our respective partners.

'I'm not sure what's going on with Ryan. He's not usually so sarcastic,' I say, thinking back on how many times he has made some ill-timed comment to something Lewis has said.

'Don't worry. Lewis just can't take a joke recently. I think he's stressed with work.'

'Ryan's the same. But will he talk about it? Not a chance. He just bottles it up and drinks another beer.'

'Yep, sounds like my husband too. Men are great at expressing their feelings in a grown-up way, aren't they?'

We both laugh before agreeing that the tension between the two men is probably nothing and that things will settle once we've all had a good night's sleep and relaxed a little more into our surroundings.

'Thanks again for inviting us up here,' I say to Kim as we each lean on the wooden beam that lines the edge of the decking area, while staring out at the rows of trees that surround most of the cabin. 'It's good to get out of the city. I mean, look at that sky. I can't remember the last time I saw the stars.'

'There's not much light pollution up here.'

'You can say that again.'

I look all around but fail to spot a single light on the horizon, only seeing the shape of the top of the trees as well as the space where the loch sits in between it all. We're so isolated here. Cut off from the world. Fully off the grid.

Those facts make me feel good in that moment.

But it won't be long until that changes, and I long to be back in civilisation again.

It's funny how quickly deceit, danger and death alter things, isn't it?

SIX

NICOLA

I'm pleased to say that things settled down after dinner and there has been no more awkwardness between Ryan and Lewis since. What there has been is a little bit of singing though, which came about after Kim mentioned she had bought a karaoke set last week and packed it because she thought it might be a fun thing for us all to do one evening during the holiday. Emily certainly agreed and she was the first person to have a go, doing her best to recite the words to a Katy Perry song as the video played on the television and the lyrics flashed up at the bottom of the screen.

Bless her, my daughter might look cute, but she hasn't been gifted with the best singing voice, not that such a thing would ever stop her from giving singing a good go, a fact I love her even more for because I wish I had her confidence when it came to such things. But I don't, which is why I have so far managed to decline all invitations to accept the microphone myself and make an attempt at singing my own version of a popular song.

'Fine, I guess it's me again,' Kim says, not as shy as me as she takes her position in front of the TV and prepares to give a rendition of her second Abba song of the night.

I admire my best friend's style and swagger as she twirls around in front of us and sings, not even needing the help from the lyrics on screen because she knows all the words and would rather look at her audience than have her back turned to us all.

The audience consists of everyone but Cole, who is still upstairs and has so far resisted all attempts from his parents to come down and join in the fun. Even Ryan went up there at one point to try and coax the teenager out, telling us he went to suggest a boys v girls competition in the hopes of getting his competitive juices flowing, but that wasn't enough to stimulate the teen and get him to socialise some more.

It seems he's no fan of karaoke, which makes two of us, but everyone else is having a great time and once Kim has finished with her latest song, Ryan leaps up from the sofa and suggests he and Lewis have a go at a duet.

'How about "Eye of the Tiger"?' he says, and Lewis seems up for the challenge, both men no doubt emboldened by the contents of the bottle of red wine they have inside themselves now, a bottle that was opened just after dinner was cleared away and a bottle that has gone some considerable way again to smoothing out the creases in their relationship.

Kim excuses herself to go to the bathroom as the two men start to sing, while I check the time and think about whether or not it's getting late for Emily to be up. It's only ten so I decide she can have a little longer yet, this being a rare holiday and all. There is still life left in this night yet, or at least I think there is until I hear the shouting from upstairs and the singing stops as we all wonder what the drama might be now.

'What's going on?' Lewis calls upstairs over the music coming from the TV.

I see Kim on the balcony above us then, emerging from Cole's bedroom with a stern look on her face, so I quickly grab the remote control and turn the volume down because, some-how, I don't think this is the time for karaoke any more.

'I've just caught your son drinking beer in his room,' Kim says, and she holds up an empty bottle to illustrate her point.

'What?' Lewis is soon stomping his way up the stairs, and I have a feeling that things aren't going to be pleasant for Cole when he gets up there. Sure enough, a big argument erupts in which Lewis demands to know why his underage son is drinking alcohol.

From what I can hear, Cole is trying to downplay the incident.

'It's just *one beer*. I'm not going to get drunk off *one beer*.'

'I told you that you couldn't have any! What part of that didn't you understand?'

I can see why Lewis might be angry but there's no need for him to shout so loudly, especially not with company. Ryan, Emily and I are right beneath them, and we can hear everything, which is hardly conducive to a relaxing holiday amongst friends.

Kim seems to realise that because she quietens her husband down as he comes out onto the balcony before saying that it's been a long day and perhaps it's time to call it a night. I couldn't agree more with that, so I tell Emily to accompany me upstairs, and while she's sad for no more singing this evening, she is old enough to know that there's enough arguments going on in this cabin without her starting one as well. It sounds like Lewis won't drop it as he is still berating his son for sneaking a beer from the fridge when all our backs were turned. At least that's what we all presume Cole did until Ryan speaks up and manages to deflect some of the blame away from the teenager.

'Go easy on him. It's my fault. I gave him the beer,' my husband admits, and I freeze on the stairs when I hear his confession.

'What?' Lewis scoffs, his icy glare bearing down on Ryan from above.

'I thought one wouldn't do any harm. Besides, he's been working hard at school, and this is his holiday too.'

Ryan might think he has a valid excuse for letting Cole have a little treat but it's not his decision to make. I know it and surely he does too. Only Lewis and Kim should decide what their son does or doesn't get.

'You had no right to do that,' Lewis says, but at least he's quite calm when he says it. 'What if he'd got sick from it? What if he was ill? We're quite far from the nearest hospital if you hadn't noticed.'

'He's not going to get sick off one beer. Besides, it's only four per cent strength. It's pretty weak.'

'That's not the point,' Kim says, and I agree with her, so I nudge Ryan and my expression urges him to apologise. But does Ryan do that? *Of course he doesn't.*

'Look, there's no harm done. Let's not fall out over it,' Ryan says, trying to downplay matters. 'You're feeling okay, aren't you, Cole?'

Cole confirms that he is, proving that there have been no adverse effects from his one beer.

'See? He's all right. He's not a full-blown alcoholic yet!'

Ryan laughs at his statement before hiccupping, a sign that he has definitely had too much wine this evening.

'Just say sorry and let's get to bed,' I whisper to him, my glare urging him to go along with that plan.

'It won't happen again,' he eventually says, which isn't quite an apology, but it seems to be the best he'll do in the circumstances.

Lewis doesn't look like he's ready to let things slide that easily, but Kim is on my side and does her own job at calming her partner down until the situation is diffused, for now at least. But there's definitely something hanging in the air of this cabin as we all make our way to our respective bedrooms to prepare for sleep, and it's certainly not laughter or music like it was earlier. It's that tension again, so palpable one could cut it with a knife, and despite trying to distract myself with Emily as I settle her down into bed, I can't shake the feeling that things aren't resolved yet. That's why once our daughter is asleep, I go to speak to my husband and ask him to apologise for what he did just then.

'Say sorry first thing in the morning,' I beg him. 'You know you're in the wrong here, right? You shouldn't have given Cole that beer. What were you thinking?'

'I was thinking that he deserved a little fun. Lord knows it doesn't sound like he has much of it, the poor boy. Not with all the tests and the maths tutors and Lewis's clear disdain for the creative subjects that Cole is obviously more interested in.'

'It's none of our business. We wouldn't want them giving things to Emily without our permission, would we?'

'That's different.'

'How is it different?'

'Emily's eleven. She's still a child.'

'So is Cole!'

'No, he's not, he's turning into an adult, and he deserves to start being treated like one.'

'Why do you care so much?'

'What do you mean?'

'I mean what has it got to do with you how Lewis and Kim treat their son? As long as they're not hurting him, which they clearly aren't, what's the problem? If they say he's too young to drink then that's that, and the last time I checked the law, he is too young to drink!'

'Arbitrary rules,' Ryan mumbles, but if that's the best he's got then I'm clearly winning this argument and he knows it. But I don't care about winning arguments. I'd rather not have any at all if I can help it. That's why I lower my voice and approach my husband, gently reaching out to him to show that what I am going to say next is more than just about me trying to one-up him.

'Please say sorry to Lewis. I'm worried about what will happen if you don't.'

'What do you mean?'

'I mean Kim's my best friend and I don't want anything to come between us, especially not our warring partners. So, please, do this for me. Say sorry and promise that you won't do anything like this again. I mean it, I don't want to lose Kim as a friend, but I'm afraid it might happen if you and Lewis don't get along.'

Ryan mellows a little at my honesty before letting out a deep sigh.

'Fine, I'll say sorry at breakfast.'

'And you won't do anything else this weekend that might antagonise Lewis?'

'It doesn't take much to antagonise him.'

'Ryan, please.'

'Okay, I won't do anything else. I swear.'

I feel a little better after receiving that assurance and I give Ryan a kiss to show him that he has finally said the right thing. If only he said the right thing all the time but show me a man who can do that and I'll be impressed.

Ryan goes into the ensuite then to brush his teeth while I remain in the bedroom and start to undress. I think about closing the curtains before I do, for extra privacy, but then remember that there's nothing out there but the odd rabbit or deer, so I don't have to worry about anybody getting a glimpse of my flesh in this semi-naked state. But I get a glimpse of something a moment later when I see the light flash on the bed.

It's a notification on a mobile phone and I realise Ryan has left his device on the duvet, so I casually glance at it to see what it might be. When I do, I see a message on the screen and the first thing I notice is the name of the person who has sent it.

It's from Kim.

I'm not sure if it's Kim as in my best friend or somebody else with the same name but a quick read through of the message gives me my answer.

I can't believe what you've been like so far. You promised not to cause trouble this weekend. Lewis and Nicola might suspect something is going on if you keep behaving like this. Please try and make more of an effort to not be so obvious.

I re-read the message a couple of times, but it still doesn't make much sense to me. Why is Kim messaging my husband and what is she talking about when she says Lewis and I might suspect something?

What's going on?

Are they having an affair?

The thought of such a thing causes my heart to start thudding in my chest and I try to tell myself that it's a ridiculous idea, but then I think about how it would explain why Ryan has been so weird with Lewis today. It's obvious there is something about Lewis that bothers my husband. I thought it was just all the money and the air of arrogance, but what if it's something else? What if it's because Lewis is with the woman who Ryan wants to be with instead?

Is that it? Is something going on between my husband and my best friend?

Judging by this text message, I'd say it most certainly is.

SEVEN

NICOLA

If there's one thing that I've learned from the past several hours, it's that there is such a thing as *too quiet*. At least that's the excuse I'm clinging on to as to why I'm struggling to sleep so much. It's like being in a vacuum here where all the sound has been sucked out and I've just been left in a silent void. No cars driving past the road outside. No voices or footsteps on the street. No bark from a dog or a clattering milk bottle disturbed by a wandering cat.

Just empty, aching silence.

I guess that's why people come to this part of Scotland. No noise pollution. Peace and quiet. *An escape.* That would be all well and good if I was in the state of mind to enjoy listening to nothing but my own thoughts, but right now that is not the case, and I have that text message to thank for that.

Ever since I saw Kim's message flash up on Ryan's phone, I have been trying to process it and figure out what it might mean. The quickest way of deciphering the true meaning behind it would have been to ask my husband outright what it was all about. But I haven't done that yet, mainly because I fear that doing so might not be the best way of getting the truth.

If I have caught him out, would he be honest with me or would he spin me a lie? Let's face it, if he is harbouring a dark secret then he's already been lying to me for quite some time now, so it wouldn't be beyond him to try and lie again. That's why I feel the best thing for me to do, to really get to the bottom of this, is to keep what I have discovered to myself for the time being and try to learn more by observing Ryan and Kim and how they interact with each other during the course of this weekend.

I've spent most of the time since we've been in Scotland watching how Ryan is with Lewis and trying to ward off another argument between the two men, so much so that I've barely paid attention to how Ryan and Kim have been with each other. But, now that I think about it, and this long night caused by an inability to sleep has made thinking the only thing I can do, there are a few things that I recall noticing about my husband and my best friend.

Of course, I'd already spotted Ryan checking out Kim as she got in and out of the hot tub in her itsy-bitsy bikini, and at the time I put that down to nothing more than him just being a typical male who was drawn to the sight of female flesh being paraded in front of him. But what if it was more than that? What if he was admiring her? Admiring what he has? What he gets to enjoy behind mine and Lewis's backs? And what if that was why Kim was so confident to wear such a skimpy outfit? Was her lack of shyness down to the fact that Ryan has already seen everything before, so covering up around him is hardly worth it now?

Then there was him offering to help Kim in the kitchen when she said she was going to make a start on dinner. Ryan never helps me prepare food at home, telling me when we first started dating that cooking was not his strong suit and that he was better off helping out with other jobs. But he tried to help Kim, though she politely declined the offer. Was that so it seemed less obvious? After all, those two working away together in the kitchen might have been an unnecessary risk.

I've been racking my brains for any other signs that the two of them might be closer than I originally thought, but barring a few compliments Ryan has made about the cabin or the food Kim prepared, all of which could be nothing more than him being polite, there is nothing that stands out. But that doesn't mean there isn't more going on beneath the surface.

The text message proves there is something there.

Ryan had no idea I saw his phone because he just came out of the ensuite and picked it up off the bed before getting beneath the duvet and telling me how tired he was. He proved it by falling asleep soon after the lights went out, and he's been sleeping like a baby ever since, unlike me who has been staring up at the ceiling while trying not to drown in a sea of paranoia.

The arrival of dawn is accompanied by the appearance of Emily in our bedroom, and she tells me that there is a deer in the back garden she has spotted from her bedroom window. I know trying to get her to go back to sleep for another hour or so is futile, so I quietly leave the bed and my sleeping husband behind and take her downstairs, where we put on our coats and shoes and go outside.

Sure enough, there is a deer outside, although he doesn't hang around for long once he sees us coming outside to get a closer look at him. The sight of the spritely animal skipping away through the forest causes Emily much excitement, but all it makes me think of is whether or not Ryan will run as fast as that away from me when I eventually confront him about whatever is going on with Kim.

'Good morning. Did you sleep well?'

My best friend's voice behind me causes me to spin around, and when I see her I wonder how she is able to look so good at this early hour and without any make-up on. I never used to envy Kim because I cared about her too much to harbour selfish feelings like that, but now it's not so easy. I'm desperate to know if she is involved with my husband, and because of that the feelings of jealousy are coming through strongly now. But not quite strongly enough for her to notice and I manage to get through five minutes of small talk about how we both slept and how peaceful it is around here during the night before Kim says she will go to make a start on breakfast.

I offer to help but she turns the offer down, something I'm pleased about because it's easier to go and sit on the sofa in my dressing gown and wallow in my drowsy state than it is to have to try and talk to her with all this on my mind. The shock and hurt over what she might have done to me is hard enough to process as it is without me having to stand beside Kim and try and fry an egg. My best friend has never done anything to damage our relationship before, so I'm having a hard time wrapping my head around the fact that she could have done something so destructive. We were the kind of friends who didn't even entertain petty arguments, either when we first linked up in our youth or as we grew older together, which is probably quite rare, but we were always above anything like that. There was never any element of competition between us. We just felt glad we had met and formed our bond.

We've been close, always have been, and I thought we always would be.

But now that whimsical belief might be as much of a joke as my marriage is.

Five minutes later and Emily is occupied enough with watching something on TV as the smell of bacon begins to fill the cabin and, thanks to the smell, it doesn't take long for our husbands to start emerging from the bedrooms and come in search of some sustenance.

Lewis comes down first and gives me a weary nod of the

head before boiling the kettle to make a cup of coffee. He mumbles a few things to Kim but only things that relate to the upkeep of this cabin, and from here they look and sound just like a typical married couple going through the motions of another early morning together. Then Ryan appears, and I keep watch on him, wondering if he steals sneaky glances at Kim and wondering if they have some sort of secret code that allows them to communicate with each other without anyone else in the room knowing about it. But I don't observe anything out of the ordinary, and the only thing my husband does once he gets downstairs is offer the apology to Lewis that is long overdue.

'I'm sorry about what happened last night. You were right, I shouldn't have given Cole that beer. I guess I'd had one too many drinks myself and thought it was a good idea. But it wasn't, obviously.'

I should be pleased that Ryan has apologised because it's what I was urging him to do while we were in the bedroom last night. But now that I know about the text message, and how Kim told him to apologise too, I'm wondering who he has done it for.

Me?

Or her?

'Don't worry about it, mate. I think we're both guilty of having a bit too much to drink last night,' Lewis replies, graciously accepting the apology, another thing that should make me happy. But now I'm worried that this man might be as gullible as I am for not thinking there is something deeper going on here just beneath the surface of all our relationships.

The apologies should signal an end to the awkwardness, but not for me because I'm still feeling on edge as I join everybody at the dining table to help myself to a big plate of bacon sandwiches and numerous jugs of fruit juice. Cole requires a little more coaxing out of his bedroom because even though the food smells good, it's still not enough to rouse a teenager from the darkest depths of sleep. Eventually, he stumbles out looking bleary-eyed and moaning about how early it is before he shoves a sandwich into his mouth and starts to wake up a little bit.

'So, what's the plan for today then?' Ryan asks cheerily as he pours himself a glass of orange juice.

'I was thinking we could go for a walk,' Kim replies, but she doesn't look at him as she answers, instead more occupied with stabbing the crispy bit of bacon on her plate with her fork. 'The weather forecast looks okay, for this morning at least, so we could get some fresh air and exercise, if that sounds okay to everyone?'

'Sounds good to me,' Lewis says as he goes to get more coffee, and everyone around this table seems to be waking up now. Everybody but me because I still feel like I'm stuck in a bad dream, one that I don't know the ending of but one that feels like it has to get worse before it eventually gets better.

'What do you think, Nic?'

Kim's question snaps me out of my trance.

'Oh, erm, yeah, a walk will be good.'

'Great! There's a trail that we can pick up not far from the cabin. It takes us through the forest and around to the loch. It's really nice, isn't it, Lew?'

Lewis confirms that it is, and with that the plan for the next part of the day is set. All of us are going to head out and do some exploring. But it's not the local area that I'm interested in learning more about. Rather, it's the true extent of my husband's relationship with my best friend. With that in mind, I will make sure to be watching and learning today. I'll be looking for more clues the pair might give away, however subtle they might be. If something is going on between them then I will figure it out.

And when I do, one thing is for sure.

This place won't be so quiet and peaceful then.

EIGHT

NICOLA

It took a while to get to the point where the six of us were ready to leave the cabin and begin our walk, and the children were the main reason for the hold up. Emily spent forever getting dressed and into the raincoat and wellies that I told her she would need to be wearing if we were going out into a muddy forest beneath a sky that always seemed to threaten rain. We've really been unlucky with the weather so far, but Kim is still adamant the weather will brighten up soon, which remains to be seen. Cole also took his sweet time in being somewhat ready to go outdoors, grumbling about having to wear boots and insisting his trainers would be fine, which was most certainly the wrong assumption and his parents had to keep reminding him of that.

Because of all the hassle, both Kim and I agreed that we missed the years when we would dress our children ourselves, back when they were much smaller and had no say or input into what covered their bodies. It seemed like a headache at the time but it turns out to be much easier than waiting for our offspring to dress themselves. But it wasn't just the kids that were delaying things. Ryan and Lewis were lethargic in their movements, no doubt due to the lingering effects of the hangover caused by last night's overindulgences. I had to speed my husband up a little after finding he was spending an age getting ready in the bathroom, and for a moment he reminded me of Cole as he sloped into the bedroom, his shoulders hunched and his mood downbeat, as if he was suddenly a teenager again and had the weight of the world on his mind.

'Maybe have a little less to drink tonight,' I suggested to him as he wearily pulled on his coat, but he didn't dignify that with an answer, never one to admit that he might have overdone it for fear of me telling him not to overdo it again.

Eventually, we were ready to leave, and as we all stepped outside onto the leaf-covered ground at the front of the cabin, the burst of cold wind that hit us told us that it would be better to keep moving if we wanted to stay warm over the next hour or so. The chilliness also takes the shine off being in such a beautiful location, and I'm guessing the sun must have been out on the day Kim and Lewis came to view this place, because otherwise they might have had second thoughts about investing here and opted for a timeshare in Spain instead.

Lewis led us to the trail that he and Kim had told us about, and as we moved along the narrow track that cut through the tall trees, the pale light from the weak sun that was poking through a few of the clouds dimmed even more beneath the canopy. Not that the lighting conditions made Ryan remove the pair of sunglasses he had opted to put on before we left. Wearing those on such a day means his hangover is even worse than I first thought, but I'm withholding my sympathy and not just because how he feels today is his own fault.

It's because I'm still suspicious of whether or not he is as good a man as I once believed him to be.

I'm reading far too much into everything that Ryan and Kim do now, including how far apart they are as we walk along this trail. Kim is ahead of me while Ryan is behind. Are those natural positions they have taken up, or are they keeping their distance, so it looks like they are less close than they really are? There hasn't been anything I've seen or heard so far today that would suggest Kim and Ryan are intimately involved. No long and lingering glances when they think no one is looking. No exchange of compliments that might seem banal but carry greater meaning. Come to think of it, there has barely been a word spoken between them.

Is that the evidence I need that something is going on? They're being so cautious to not give themselves away that they're almost at the point of completely ignoring each other, which is doing the opposite. But maybe I'm just reading far too much into things? One thing I do know is all this overthinking is driving me mad, so I try and relax for a moment and that's something that isn't too hard to do in a setting like this one.

'They look like Christmas trees!' Emily cries as she points at the pines that surround us on both sides, and my little girl is right. They do look like Christmas trees and just the mention of the C-word is enough to make me mentally calculate how many weeks it is until the big day and think about how much I have to do before it arrives.

It always comes round so fast, doesn't it?

The sound of a babbling brook nearby causes Emily to run ahead and once we've caught her up, we find her throwing sticks into a small stream of water. I take out my phone to snap a picture of her and she smiles at me because she has always been one to enjoy the attention of a camera. Kim asks Cole if he would pose for a photo as well, but he isn't as enthusiastic as Emily and keeps walking on, clearly preferring his own company to everyone else's.

'Get as many photos while you can,' Kim advises me as she forlornly puts her phone back in her pocket. 'I can't remember the last time I got Cole to stand still for a picture.'

The advice might be helpful but all I am thinking is whether or not she could give me any advice on how to keep a man happy, and more specifically my man. If she is having an affair with him then she must know the secret to that particular question, and it would also mean she would know where I am going wrong with him.

Has Ryan got bored of me while Kim has found a way of exciting him?

I need to know, and I start to entertain the idea of asking my husband outright about the message I saw as soon as we are alone together again. But out here in the wild isn't the time or the place so I keep quiet as we carry on walking, and after spotting a couple of deer grazing in the forest, we make it to the banks of the loch, the same one that we can see from the hot tub.

The water is still and calm, the polar opposite of my mental state, but Cole tosses a chunky rock into the loch a moment later and the disruptive ripples it sends out in all directions as it plunges to the bottom are far more representative of my brainwaves at this particular time.

'Here, have a go at this,' Ryan says and he expertly skims a stone across the surface of the loch, watching it as it bounces away before eventually slowing down and succumbing to gravity, dropping beneath the surface but with much less disturbance than Cole's rock did.

'How did you do that?' Cole asks as he tries and fails to get his own stone to skim, and Ryan teaches him, once again displaying his easy way with a young boy and making me wonder how much he regrets me not being able to give him a son.

Could that be the reason he has strayed? Does he harbour all sorts of animosity to me, animosity that has eventually manifested in him cheating on me with my best friend? That would be extremely callous because it's not my fault I gave birth to a girl and not a boy, just like it's not my fault we had no luck conceiving again. Is Ryan really that bitter and is he really capable of being so vengeful? Or am I once again reading far too much into things?

I think I might be when I see Ryan teaching Emily how to skim a stone too, because he is just as caring and compassionate with her, proving that he loves his daughter and invalidating that particular fear that he might love a boy more than a girl. I see even more proof when Emily is successful in getting her stone to skip across the top of the water and Ryan celebrates by lifting her up and spinning her around, causing her to giggle loudly and beg her daddy to put her down.

Seeing how good a father Ryan is to our child makes me feel even more afraid of what his secret might be because I don't want to stop thinking of him as the perfect husband and dad. I'd hate for him to just be labelled like all the other men who have betrayed their families, although that might be his fate if I unravel his lies.

'A cheating scumbag.'

'A waste of space.'

'Just like all the others.'

That's what people might say about him if they found out he was having an affair, and it's what I might say too. Those things are in stark contrast to what people currently say about him.

'He's such a nice guy.'

'You've got yourself a good one there.'

'Where can I find myself a man like him?'

I've heard other women say all those things and more about Ryan over the years, but my heart almost skips a beat when I think of that last one because I can remember who the person was that said it. It was Kim. She asked me where she could find a man like Ryan not long after I had started dating him and after I'd told her all about how romantic and affectionate he was with me. I didn't think anything of it at the time because it's just the kind of thing friends say when one of their group enters into a relationship and is positively glowing about how good it is. It's just a light-hearted, jokey thing to say, and I'm sure I've said it to other people before when they have been waxing lyrical about their latest partner. But what if Kim didn't say it as just a throwaway remark? What if she actually meant it? What if telling her all about Ryan in the early stages of our relationship made her attracted to him, and once she met him that attraction only grew?

'Are you okay? You look a bit pale.'

Kim has a look of concern on her face as she waits for me to answer her, and everyone else stops what they are doing as well, more interested in what might be wrong with me than they are in skimming any more stones across this loch.

'I'm fine!' I lie before realising I need to say something more if I'm to deflect the attention fully away from myself. 'I'm just a little cold.'

'It is chilly. Let's keep walking,' Kim suggests, but the thought of heading deeper into this forest is not a pleasant one because all I want to do is get back to the cabin and have a moment alone. Maybe lock myself in the bathroom and put my head between my knees or maybe even take a pillow in there with me so I can scream into it. Anything to stop these damn thoughts from overwhelming me.

It's as if I receive a little divine intervention then because we've barely moved a few more yards down the trail when we start to feel raindrops hitting our skin. Looking up, we notice that the sky has gone dark again and what little bit of sun we saw earlier is now completely hidden behind thick clouds that are clearly carrying a lot of rain.

So much for summer.

'I think we should head back,' Lewis suggests, and I can't agree with him quickly enough.

Emily isn't happy about that plan and even Cole says he'd rather stay out, but the rumble of thunder they hear a moment later soon has them agreeing that taking shelter is the more sensible option at present.

The walk back to the cabin is a brisk one and by the time we make it back, we're all completely soaked, the storm catching us before we could take cover and almost mocking the flimsy raincoats that we all thought might be up to the task today. But at least we're back, and as the cabin door closes behind us and Lewis makes a start on getting the fire going, I can't shake a grim thought. It's the thought that says the next time we all leave this place together, our relationships will never be the same again.

NINE

NICOLA

The roaring fire that I am staring into might be warming my skin but now there is an icy coldness to my character that I fear might never thaw out.

Not if I find out that I've been lied to.

'Is it too early to open a bottle of wine?' Lewis asks me once he has stopped prodding the stacks of wood in the fire with a poker, satisfied that it will be burning for a while now.

Considering that it's only one o'clock in the afternoon, I'd normally say yes it is but also considering my mental anguish, the only answer I can give today is a no.

'Go for it,' I tell Lewis and he doesn't need much persuading, getting up quickly and procuring a bottle of red from inside one of the many cupboards in the kitchen.

It's just the two of us down here at the moment. Ryan and Emily are in their respective bathrooms, while Kim is in her shower, telling us before she went in that the only thing that makes up for being soaked in cold water outside is being soaked by warm water inside. As for Cole, I presume he's in his room again, possibly feeling like he's already fulfilled his 'socialising' quota for one day. That just leaves Lewis and I down here.

Neither of us could be bothered showering, preferring just to quickly change our clothes before settling in front of the fire. But now we are alone, if only for a few more minutes, I wonder if it might be a good time to ask him if everything is okay, as far as his marriage is concerned, and particularly try and figure out if he has any doubts about his partner's loyalty like I have about mine.

'Let me give you a hand with that,' I say, joining him in the kitchen and picking up the bottle opener while he takes out four wine glasses.

I dig the corkscrew into the top of the bottle and begin working on removing the cork, a task that isn't too difficult because I've opened more than my fair share of bottles in the past, not just for pleasure but because I spent a couple of years working as a waitress in a fancy French restaurant in my early twenties. While that job was just one in a long list of tedious forms of employment for me, it does remind me of a more care-free time. A time when all I needed to worry about was covering my rent and figuring out what to do on my days off. It was also the time when I was sharing a flat with Kim and we had plenty of fun together.

I really hope those precious memories can remain intact and untainted.

But that remains to be seen.

'Cheers,' Lewis says as I start to pour, and once we have a glass each we take our seats on the sofa and bask in the warmth of the fire again. But the footsteps we can hear on the floor-boards above us remind me that it won't be long before our partners are back with us, so I cut to the chase.

'How's everything with you and Kim?' I ask, doing my best to make it sound like a casual question rather than a loaded one.

'Huh?'

'Are you good?'

'Yeah. Why wouldn't we be?'

'Oh, no reason. I'm just thinking because you've got a teenage son, a busy business and most likely not enough hours in the day to do everything you need to. It must be quite tough to make time for each other.'

'Yeah, I guess. But we manage.'

I'm not sure if Lewis is being completely honest with me or is too distracted by the wine and the fire to go a little deeper with his answers, so I change tact slightly.

'Please don't say anything to Kim but I've noticed she's been a little different lately.'

'What do you mean?'

'I don't know. A little distracted, maybe. No, that's not it. A little less open with me, yeah, that's what I mean.'

'Less open?'

'You know, just not her usual chatty self. I was worried something was wrong.'

'I don't think so.'

'You haven't noticed anything like that? She hasn't been different with you in any way?'

I'm trying to ascertain whether or not Kim has changed her behaviour around her husband. Become more secretive? Less available? Making excuses? Perhaps spending less time with him and more time somewhere else? But if she has then Lewis hasn't noticed it.

'No, not that I'm aware of,' he tells me with a shrug. 'Same old Kim as far as I can tell.'

This could be the point where I lose patience with dancing around the subject and just come out with what's really on my mind, asking Lewis if he thinks it might be possible that his wife is having an affair with Ryan. But such a question seems outrageous to utter out loud and it would be like opening Pandora's box, letting things out that could never be forgotten. Then there's the fact that Ryan is coming back downstairs now so I've missed my chance anyway, and I quietly remind Lewis not to mention what we just talked about to Kim before I tell my husband there is wine available in the kitchen.

'Great,' he says as he helps himself while telling me that Emily is snuggled up under her duvet reading a Harry Potter book, so she won't be bothering us for a while.

With Ryan joining us, the two men discuss the merits of a good fire and how satisfying it is to build one because isn't that what all men do whenever they're in front of a fireplace? As for me, I wait for Kim to come back downstairs, all the time wondering if she might have sent my husband another text message since that last one or, better yet, spoken to him quietly upstairs when Ryan was up there a moment ago.

The idea of the pair of them in cahoots with each other makes me angry and sad at the same time but I've no way of knowing, have I? Not unless I can get Ryan's phone again and check it, which is not an easy task because he has it on his person almost all the time; that one rare occasion yesterday when he didn't provided me with a brief glimpse into what really goes on in his world. Unless I can somehow eavesdrop on a private conversation between Ryan and Kim, then I will never know what they might be talking about behind closed doors.

But that doesn't mean I'm not going to keep looking for an opportunity.

When Kim appears, she looks immaculate, her hair dried and pristine again and she even found the time to apply a little make-up, which makes me feel even more of a slob compared to her as I sit here in my jogging bottoms and a baggy T-shirt, holding a rather large glass of wine in the early afternoon.

'Cole's in a mood because there's no phone signal,' she tells us, letting us know that it will just be us adults then for the foreseeable future. 'He said he wanted to call a friend, but he can't, so that means it's all my fault, of course.'

'Would that be a female friend by any chance?' Ryan asks, raising his eyebrows at Cole's parents.

'Not that we know of,' Lewis scoffs. 'We haven't heard him mention any girlfriends yet, have we, Kim?'

'Well, no, but he's not likely to tell us about them, is he?' she says as she joins us, forgoing her own glass of wine for the time being and opting for a banana instead, which gives me another reason to feel inferior.

'I bet he's got loads of girls on the go,' Ryan says with a smirk. 'I know I did at his age.'

'Oh, did you now?' I ask, giving his ribcage a nudge with my elbow.

'I don't think he has,' Lewis says, not entertaining the humorous suggestion. 'He's got enough on his plate with his schoolwork and figuring out what he wants to do next, not that it should require much thought.'

'What do you mean?' I ask.

'Well, it's obvious what he should do when he finishes school. He should join my business and work for me.'

'What if he doesn't want to do that?'

Ryan's question might be a simple one, but it comes across as quite blunt when he voices it, and Lewis doesn't look too impressed.

'What do you mean? Of course he wants to.'

'But it sounds like he isn't sure what he wants to do yet. Have you asked him?'

'I don't see why he wouldn't want to work with me. He's got a readymade job he can walk straight into from school. I wish I had had that opportunity when I was his age. It would have saved me a lot of years of struggling before I got up and running.'

'Yeah, but everyone's different, aren't they? He should probably figure it out on his own.'

'Who really knows what they want to do at that age?' Lewis scoffs. 'I mean, if I asked him, he'd say he wants to be a footballer, but that's hardly realistic.'

'Yeah, better to play it safe and not follow a dream, I suppose,' Ryan replies, his sarcastic side back with a vengeance.

I can sense that Ryan and Lewis are on the verge of another disagreement, but unlike yesterday I'm not going to try and stop it before it gets going. That's because I'm no longer as worried about keeping things civil for the sake of mine and Kim's friendship, a friendship that might not be as valuable as I once thought. So that's why I sit back and just take another sip from my wine glass to see how this plays out, although Kim does make an attempt at nipping it in the bud.

'It's a while before Cole takes his exams and has to think about what he does next, so let's not try and worry about it too much yet, okay?' she says before tossing her banana peel onto the log table behind the sofa.

But the men don't take the hint and carry on their discussion.

'There's nothing wrong with doing something practical careerwise,' Lewis says. 'It hasn't done me any harm. Look at this cabin it's afforded me.'

'I'm just saying Cole might have other ambitions. Things he wants to explore. A job will always be waiting for him once he's tried all that, I'm sure.'

'Sounds like you're an advocate of wasting time. But you are the only one out of us four who went to university, aren't you, so I guess that makes sense. Easier to be a student than a contributing member of society.'

'Oh, I don't know. If you're asking me whether it's better for a teenager to venture out by themselves into the world and have fun with friends or sit behind a desk pushing papers in some dreary office then I think I know which is more fulfilling.'

It really seems like Ryan and Lewis are content to keep voicing their opinion, regardless of what damaging things might be said if they carry on down this path. I'm all for it because it's about time things got out in the open here and if this is the way for it to happen then so be it.

Kim intervenes, getting up and telling Lewis to come with her to get the hot tub ready for its next use, and despite him being mid-debate she is successful at extracting him from the room, leaving Ryan and I on the sofa.

'What's gotten into you?' I ask him. 'Why are you always picking fights with Lewis?'

'I'm not picking fights.'

'You disagree with everything he says.'

'Am I not allowed to have my own opinion?'

'Not when it causes arguments between friends.'

'Yeah, well, maybe we're not friends.'

'What do you mean by that?'

'I'm just saying, I only hang out with him because you're seeing Kim.'

'So you don't like him? Why?'

Is it because he is married to the woman you are secretly sleeping with?

'Just forget it,' Ryan replies, getting up and heading upstairs. 'I'm going to check on Emily. Give me a shout when the hot tub's ready.'

He leaves me alone then, still not having really given me much insight into why everything Lewis seems to say gets on his nerves. But it's clear that the pressure cooker of this cabin is pushing him to his limits. The same goes for Lewis, too, and judging by how quick Kim was to leave the room just now, I'm guessing she is struggling as well. That makes me think it is only a matter of time before one of them cracks and maybe then I'll get the real story.

I just need something to happen to cause the tipping point.

Little did I know then, I was just about to get it.

TEN

COLE

My mum's just been in my room to ask me if I wanted to get in the hot tub with everyone else.

What an invitation. Getting half-naked with my parents and their crusty friends.

Erm, let me think about that one.

No, thanks.

Mum wasn't happy that I've chosen to stay in my room rather than come down and 'socialise' but what does she expect? How am I meant to socialise with people I don't have anything in common with?

I'm not anti-social at all. I love hanging out with my friends, having a laugh, having a beer in the park, maybe enjoy a cheeky cigarette too. But none of my friends are here and I'm not allowed to smoke or drink around Mum and Dad, so this is not my idea of socialising.

I wish there was somebody here who was my age but the closest is Emily and she's only eleven. She's still a kid. But I'm not a kid anymore. I'm ready to do my own thing now.

I just wish Mum and Dad would realise that and leave me to it.

The frustration that I seem to feel on a daily basis rises up inside me again and I throw the football magazine I brought with me on this trip against the wardrobe opposite my bed. It makes a loud noise as it hits the wood before falling to the floor, but I doubt anyone else heard it because they're all outside on the decking. I can hear them down below through my open window, talking and laughing, having whatever boring conversations they might be having and not caring that they've dragged me here and made me miserable.

I didn't want to come. I would have been perfectly happy staying by myself at home. Obviously, I would have secretly had a house party while my parents were away, and it would have been epic but that hasn't been allowed to happen. That's because I'm stuck here now in bloody Scotland, bored out of my mind.

I can't even use my phone because there's no internet. What a joke. I could kill loads of time on social media but not without Wi-Fi. And I can't even call anybody because there's no signal either.

I'm annoyed because I was supposed to call Rebecca, one of the girls from my school. We swapped numbers in the park last weekend, when a few of our friends had met to have a few drinks behind the bushes where no one can catch us. I've fancied Rebecca for ages, so I was glad I got her number, and I was looking forward to talking to her today. I guess we would have chatted for a bit about stuff we're into, and she might have told me about a party one of her mates is having soon that I could have gone to with my friends. But no, I can't talk to her now because we're in this stupid place that's like being back in the dark ages.

Damn Mum and Dad. They're always getting in the way of my fun. At least they don't know about Rebecca, and I'll keep it that way. They'll only embarrass me if they find out that I like someone. They'll probably want to invite her for dinner and ask her all sorts of questions. Urgh, horrible. I have to make sure they never meet her.

I pick up my phone to have another go at getting online, but the symbol in the top corner of the screen is still showing me that there's no signal or Wi-Fi connection. All I can use my phone for now is to listen to music, so I try that but I'm barely one minute into a song before I get the 'Low Battery' bleep to tell me I need to charge it.

I get up and grab my rucksack and rummage through it looking for my charger. But it's not here. Damn it, where is it? I'm sure I packed it. Then again, maybe I forgot. I'm always forgetting something. Oh no, my phone's going to die in a minute and then I'll really have nothing to do.

I think about asking Mum or Dad for their charger, but that would mean going out to the hot tub and I bet they wouldn't give me what I want. They'd just tell me to join them, which is the last thing I want to do, so I'm better off staying away from them. They seem to have forgotten about me for now so at least they aren't bothering me, and I'll enjoy it while it lasts because it never lasts long.

I do need a way of listening to some music to stop me completely dying of boredom, so I leave my bedroom and wander between the other rooms on the lookout for another phone charger that I could steal. But I can't see one anywhere, not even downstairs. I find Dad's car keys on the kitchen counter and I know he has a charging cable in his car, so I swipe the keys and head outside.

I go to where the car is parked at the front of the cabin, well away from everybody else in the hot tub at the back of the cabin, and once I've unlocked the car I get inside. No sooner am I behind the wheel then I'm thinking about how I can't wait to turn seventeen so I can get a car of my own. Then there'll be no stopping me. I could go anywhere I want to at any time.

See you later, Mum and Dad.

I find the charging cable and am just about to pull it out of its socket and take it inside when I can't resist the temptation to put the key in the ignition. What if I started the engine and took this thing for a joyride? It would be easy. There are no other cars around here. I could just drive down the track to the main road and then come back. Mum and Dad wouldn't even know that I was gone.

But knowing my luck, they'd find out and I'd get in a load of trouble, so I won't bother. I also don't really know how to drive, so there's a chance I might crash and while I'm not worried about getting hurt, I am worried about damaging this car so we can't drive out of here and go home soon.

Imagine being stuck here for even more time.

Horrendous.

I think about taking the key back out of the ignition and just going back inside to my room, but the thought of being cooped up in there all afternoon is horrible, so I figure I might just stay here. With the key in the ignition and the engine off, the charger works, so I plug my phone in and with the extra battery life, the music starts to play again.

I recline the seat and lie back, relaxing with the driver's side door open beside me so I get some fresh air, and this is much better than being in that stuffy room upstairs.

It's so comfortable that I feel like I could drift off to sleep, and as one of my favourite songs starts to play I think I just might.

Unfortunately, I'm going to regret it when I wake up.

ELEVEN

NICOLA

The incessant bubbling of the water all around me in this tub is akin to the constant churning of the thoughts in my mind as I sip from a glass of champagne and try to enjoy myself. I'm seated beside Ryan while Kim and Lewis are sitting opposite us. Emily is in between, bobbing about in the water, all of her body besides her head submerged whereas the adults have the tops of their shoulders out, such are the slightly cramped conditions in this tub.

Lewis says it can hold six adults, but I'd say that's an exaggeration. We're relatively squashed in as it is, but at least there is a small distance between my husband and my best friend, or at least there is above the water anyway. But what might be going on beneath it? Might their legs be brushing against one another's? Could there be a wandering hand touching an ankle or a thigh? It's possible and without being able to see what might be happening under the water, I can't help but think how Ryan and Kim could be getting away with something so wrong right under mine and Lewis's noses.

'We've got to get one of these at home,' Ryan remarks, referring to the hot tub that he is clearly enjoying soaking in.

'We don't have the space,' I remind him. 'Or the budget.'

'We could make it work,' he replies casually and the fact he has stopped being practical tells me that the bubbles in the champagne have started going to his head. It's champagne that needs replenishing because our current bottle has just run dry, and Ryan is only too eager to get some more.

He gets out of the tub and heads inside to the fridge, offering to go so that no one else has to subject themselves to the cold air that hits them as soon as they leave the comfort of the warm water behind.

With him gone temporarily, I have a bit more room to stretch out and I get even more when Lewis says he is going to visit the men's room.

'Check on Cole while you're there,' Kim tells him. 'He can't stay in his room all day.'

Lewis confirms that he will give their son another reminder about the virtues of coming outside to converse with other people before he enters the cabin too, leaving us girls in the tub.

'Look, Mummy. My hands are all wrinkly,' Emily says, showing me her water-weathered hands.

'Yeah, you'll have to get out soon,' I tell my daughter, but she doesn't like the sound of that.

'The men seem to be getting along again,' Kim says as she waits for her empty glass to be refilled. 'That's a relief.'

'Yeah, it is. But something still isn't right. Are you sure you don't know what it might be?'

Another chance for somebody to tell me the truth here.

But another chance that goes begging.

'Beats me. Boys being boys, I suppose. A need to win an argument. I thought that was just us who needed to do that but we're definitely not as bad as them.'

Kim looks so cool sitting opposite me in this tub. So in control. Assured. As if she doesn't have a care in the world. But I know she does because I saw her message last night.

She has problems and she has secrets. She is just clearly very good at covering it up. But nothing stays buried forever.

Ryan reappears on the decking and pops the cork out of a new bottle of champagne, causing it to hit the underside of the decking roof and make an almighty bang.

'Oops, sorry about that. Don't tell Lewis,' Ryan says with a daft smirk, and Kim tells him not to worry about it.

He tops up both of our glasses before getting back into the tub, but when he does, he doesn't sit beside me this time. *He sits beside her.*

Is he really going to be that obvious? If so, then maybe it's time for me to be obvious too. But to ask the question that I'm dying to ask, I need to remove Emily from the situation.

'I think you should get out,' I tell my daughter. 'Go and dry off. I'll be in shortly.'

'But Mum, I don't want to!'

'Come on, don't be silly now. It's time to get out.'

'Leave her, she's okay,' Ryan says, sitting back in the tub with his arms outstretched behind Kim and looking as assured as she does.

'No, it's time for her to get out and I'd appreciate it if you helped me,' I say, letting Ryan know I'm not in the mood for him being an unhelpful parent right now.

He gets the message and tells Emily to start drying off, and after a little more moaning from her she does as he says, leaving the tub and running into the cabin, shivering as she goes but at least she's out of the way.

'I need to ask you both something,' I say, fixing Ryan and Kim with a steely glare. 'And I need you to tell me the truth.'

All of a sudden, neither of them looks particularly assured any more. And they look even less so when I ask the question.

'What's going on between you two?'

The only noise then is the sound of the bubbles all around

us but I'm not going to speak again. The ball is in their court now.

It's Kim who has the decency to reply first, although not quite the decency to answer honestly.

'What do you mean? There's nothing going on.'

'Yeah, we're not sure what you're talking about,' Ryan says, laughing a little albeit very nervously.

'Oh, come on, guys, at least do me the courtesy of being honest with me. I'm your wife. And I'm your best friend. Or at least I thought I was.'

Another awkward silence but I've left the pair with nothing to say but the truth now because they surely know that I'm onto them and whatever has been happening behind my back.

'Nic, I'm not sure what you want me to tell you,' Kim starts.

'How about the truth.'

'What truth?'

The door to the cabin suddenly opens and Lewis appears before telling me that Emily is asking for me.

'Just one moment!' I reply and I look back to Kim and Ryan to show them that I'm not finished with them yet.

'No, she really needs you. She's upset,' Lewis tells me.

'What?'

My daughter being in distress is about the only thing that could tear me away from this conversation, and I leave the hot tub without hearing what I needed to. But that doesn't mean I won't pick up where I left off when I get back.

'She's upstairs in the main bathroom,' Lewis tells me as I go inside. 'Have you seen Cole by the way?'

'No,' I say, and he goes in search of his son while I go upstairs, worried about my daughter but also worried about the fact that I've just left Kim and Ryan alone in the tub. It seems ridiculous to feel like I can't trust the pair of them to be left by themselves for a few minutes but that's what it's come to and it's a sad indictment of things. The image of the two of them kissing in the bubbling hot water flashes across my mind and is a very unwelcome one, but even as I dismiss it I can't easily shake off the feeling of dread that accompanies it.

I reach the bathroom door as quickly as I can but find it locked, so I knock.

'Emily? Is everything okay?'

'No,' comes the feeble reply.

'What's happened?'

'I don't know.'

'Open the door and let me in.'

'No.'

'I can't help you if you don't let me in.'

I get no response so I'm not sure what is happening until I hear the sound of the lock twisting. The door is now open, so I go inside and when I do I find my daughter looking very sad and confused.

'What is it?' I ask again, afraid because I've never seen her looking like this.

Emily doesn't reply, just pointing to the toilet instead, so I go over to check it and when I look inside the bowl I see the water inside it is a murky red colour.

'I think I'm ill,' Emily says quietly behind me but she's wrong and that's a relief.

'You're not ill, darling,' I reassure her.

'Then what is it?'

'It's your period,' I tell her, putting a comforting arm around her small shoulders to let her know that this is not something to be afraid of.

'What?'

Emily looks confused and that makes me regret not broaching this subject with her sooner because it was inevitable that it would have to be discussed one day. From what I remember of my own experience, as well as a little research online recently, the average age for this to start is eleven, which means Emily is right on time. But of course, that won't be much consolation to a little girl who has experienced a simple trip to the toilet suddenly turning into a scary event.

I flush the toilet before locking the bathroom door so that we can't be interrupted. Then I quietly explain to my little girl what is going on with her body and how the changes she is experiencing mean she is slowly but surely growing into a woman.

She understands it, at least for the most part, mentioning that she recalls hearing something about it at school, but while she is still a little uncertain, she is mainly relieved that she isn't dying. That's something I reassure her about one more time before she stops giving me her worried look. Then I explain how we can buy certain things to help her with this bodily function and that it's something I go through myself, which makes her feel better. I also offer her use of some of those aforementioned things to help her in the moment, which allows a little of her curiosity to replace her fear and angst.

'You'll be okay,' I tell her. 'But for the time being, just let me know when you need to go to the toilet and we'll deal with this together, all right?'

'Okay,' she replies, and I give her a hug before asking if she is ready to leave the bathroom.

Emily nods her head so I unlock the door and tell her I'll meet her in her bedroom in a moment but need to use the toilet myself first. I lock the door again and return to the bowl and I'm just about to start my business when I hear Ryan's voice nearby. But it's not coming from inside the cabin. It's outside and, more specifically, via the window that is open in this room. The bathroom is directly above the hot tub so I can hear what he is saying to Kim down below, and as I stand by the window and lean a little closer, I hear a lot more.

'She obviously knows something,' Ryan says, his voice hushed but urgent. 'The question is how?'

'I have no idea,' Kim replies. 'I haven't said anything.'

'Neither have I!'

'Maybe she doesn't know then. Maybe she is talking about something else. It might be about you and Lewis arguing all the time.'

'No, it's not that. She had a look in her eye. This is more serious. She is onto us.'

'Impossible.'

'Is it? She's not stupid. We always knew there was a chance she would find out.'

'But she can't have found out! We've been careful!'

'She obviously knows something. You heard what she asked us. She asked for the truth.'

'What are we supposed to say?'

'I don't know!'

It's clear now. They're definitely having an affair. As soon as I'm done in here, I'm going to go downstairs, tell them the game is up and then ask Lewis to drive Emily and I out of here.

At least that was the plan until I heard what my husband said next.

'She can't find out that Cole is mine. She'd leave me. The fact that she hasn't done so yet might mean she doesn't know everything.'

What?

Cole is his?

It's a good job this window isn't open any more or I'd be in danger of toppling out of it because I suddenly feel very faint.

My husband is Cole's dad? Is that what he just said? If so, why the hell hasn't Kim corrected him? Cole is Lewis's, not Ryan's.

Right?

'Maybe we just need to go home,' Kim says then. 'Come up

with an excuse why we need to leave. Say you have to do something for work or whatever. I'm sure Lewis won't mind leaving early, he's hardly having fun. We can just get out of here and Nicola can't ask us any more questions then. She obviously won't ask in front of the kids.'

'Maybe.'

'No, that's what we have to do. We need to leave. Now.'

I peep out and see Kim and Ryan getting out of the hot tub below me then, wrapping themselves in towels before going inside. They think they can get away with this. They think they can just cut the weekend short, and their secret will stay safe. But that's not going to happen. I can expose them.

All I need to do is get my legs working.

It's stupid but I can't move. I feel so weak after what I just heard that my body feels like it's shutting down.

Ryan is Cole's dad. That means he slept with Kim and not recently either. Almost sixteen years ago. That means it would have been at the start of our marriage. That was a time when we were trying to conceive ourselves, a time when we had no idea it was going to take us over four long years to have Emily.

He cheated on me. They both did.

And Cole is the result.

Thinking about such a terrible thing means it's easy for my paranoia to go into overdrive then. The more afraid I get, the scarier the questions are that come to mind.

Has something been going on between Kim and Ryan all this time? Oh God, what if they have been at it for years? Has my whole marriage been a sham? Was Ryan sleeping with Kim while I was pregnant with Emily? With what I know now, it's not hard for me to imagine him going to her while I was lying at home in bed with a swollen stomach complaining about feeling sick. *I feel like I could be sick right now.*

I rush back to the toilet and lean over it, holding my hair back as I prepare to gag. But just before anything comes up, I hear shouting from downstairs. It's Lewis and he sounds angry about something.

Did he overhear Kim and Ryan too?

Has he just uncovered the horrific truth about Cole like I have?

If so, I dread to think what he might do now.

TWELVE

NICOLA

I emerge from the bathroom like a defeated and punch-drunk boxer leaving the ring. I'm dazed, confused, worried about what my future holds, and all while still not quite sure what just happened.

I can't believe what I just heard, and I don't know if I ever will fully be able to comprehend it. This is far worse than I imagined. I just thought Ryan and Kim were having an affair.

If only that was the extent of this nightmare.

I can still hear Lewis shouting downstairs, so I look over the edge of the balcony that gives me a view of the lounge area and kitchen below, but fail to see him or anybody else. That might be a good thing because if I caught another glimpse of Ryan or Kim then it might make me go running back into the bathroom to try and be sick again.

The noise continues and I figure Lewis is outside some-where, so I tentatively head down the stairs, my hand clutching the banister as I go because I'm still feeling weak and my legs could give out from underneath me at any time. But by the time I've reached the bottom step, I've figured out exactly where the shouting is coming from.

It's the front of the cabin and when I look through the glass doors, I see Lewis out there. But he's not by himself.

Ryan, Kim and Cole are there too.

I have no idea how I am supposed to face those three, not with what I know about them all now. But maybe Lewis is shouting because he knows too.

What else could it be?

I open the door and step outside, but nobody notices my appearance. That's because they all have their backs to me and seem to be focused on Lewis and Kim's car.

'You stupid idiot! How are we supposed to drive out of here now?'

Lewis is fuming and I can actually see a bulging vein on the side of his neck as he berates Cole, who is standing awkwardly by the open driver's side door.

Lewis is sitting behind the wheel of the car and he turns the keys, trying to initiate the engine but it just makes a feeble sound that tells everyone here this car isn't going anywhere.

'What's happened?' I ask, and Kim and Ryan turn to see me standing behind them, resulting in another wave of nausea passing through me.

'I'll tell you what's happened. This idiot has only gone and drained the battery!' Lewis cries, pointing at the ashen-faced Cole, who looks like he's on the verge of tears, either because of the silly mistake he has made or maybe just because of the berating he is taking from his father.

Except he's not really his father, is he? Cole's real dad is standing a few yards away from him, and he's wearing a wedding ring that I helped him put on in front of all our family and friends. But I'm guessing Cole has no idea about who his real father is either, neither does Lewis because if he did then he'd surely be more frustrated about that than he is about the problem with the car.

'How long did you have the key in the ignition for?' Lewis asks Cole as he keeps trying and failing to start the engine.

'I don't know.'

'Yeah, you don't know because you fell asleep. Seriously, how stupid can you be?'

'Hey, come on. It was an accident.'

But that attempt at a defence didn't come from Cole. It came from Ryan. He's sticking up for the boy.

He's sticking up for his son.

It's as if the veil has suddenly been lifted from over my eyes and now I see everything so clearly. All the times Ryan argued Cole's side of things in discussions with Lewis, including about what the youngster should do with his life after school. I just thought Ryan was trying to offer a balanced argument or was just showing a little bit of compassion for the teenager. But now I know there was so much more to it than that. Ryan was always telling Lewis to go easier on Cole not because he was just being nice but because he genuinely cared about him, and he cared because he knew he was his own flesh and blood.

All the arguments and disagreements Ryan had with Lewis. All the silly quarrels and games of one-upmanship. All the times I thought it was just because Lewis got on Ryan's nerves so I would ask my husband to try and relax. No wonder Ryan couldn't do it. No wonder he had to engage with Lewis on occasion. It was because he was trying to cope with the fact that another man was raising his son right in front of his eyes. It must have been torture for him. But does that mean I have sympathy and feel sorry for him?

Not one bit.

I have a good mind to storm over to my husband now and slap him across the face before doing the same thing to the woman standing next to him. Both of them deserve to be punished for the terrible secret they have harboured all this time, and I'm not the only one who deserves to get a measure of revenge. Lewis does too, that poor man might be a little arrogant and pretentious when it comes to business and money, but he definitely does not deserve to have been lied to about the true origins of the child that he has spent fifteen years looking after.

I should tell Lewis now. Really get this out in the open. Blow the lid off this whole sordid affair. But then I look at Cole again, standing there so uselessly beside the car, still being scolded for foolishly leaving the key in the ignition to the point that he completely drained the battery, and I can't do it. I can't pile on the misery for this poor boy. It wouldn't be fair. How the hell is he supposed to process the fact that his whole life has been a lie? How will he react to finding out he has a different dad? He deserves to know the truth, of course he does, but he also deserves to find out in a more dignified way than me just shouting it as we all stand around this car outside this damn cabin.

The same goes for me telling Lewis too. I need to do it but not here, not in these circumstances because I can't predict his reaction, although I expect it to be a violent one based on how he seems to react to everything else that goes wrong for him. Assuming he does react badly, a reaction that would be totally justified, I realise we're in possibly the worst place for such a reaction to occur.

Stranded here, in the middle of nowhere, with a broken down car and nothing and no one else around us for miles. There would be no way for any of us to get away and process our thoughts and feelings about this in a less stress-free environment. We'd just be trapped with each other and that would only make things a whole lot worse.

So I don't say anything. Not yet. Not until Lewis can fix this car and we have the chance to get the hell out of here. But it doesn't seem like such a thing is going to happen anytime soon because after trying the engine several more times without success, Lewis gives up and slams his hands against the steering wheel.

'It's no good. It's completely dead. We can't drive this car in this state.'

The grim verdict was one we were all probably expecting when we found out what had happened but it's still sobering when we hear it spoken out loud, nonetheless. That's because it confirms the predicament we are in now.

We are stuck in the middle of a forest in the Scottish Highlands with no phone signal, internet connection or mode of transport to take us back to civilisation.

I might have been forgiven for thinking things couldn't get much worse than finding out that my husband and my best friend had slept together and conceived a child who they had passed off as another man's for fifteen years.

But somehow, things have gotten worse.

That's because I'm now trapped with those people.

And I have no idea how I'm going to get away from them before I do something I regret.

THIRTEEN

NICOLA

How long should a person keep trying before they give up and admit they're fighting a losing cause? Minutes? Hours? Never? I'm watching Lewis continue to battle vainly with the car key in trying to engage the engine, but I could also be referring to my marriage and how that might now be just as hopeless a cause as getting this car back on the road without a mechanic's help.

Is it even worth trying to talk all of this through with Ryan, to give him the chance to offer some kind of explanation as to how and why he came to father a child with my best friend? Or should I just throw up my hands and declare it all over? Lewis has finally done this now, as he gets out of the car, slams the driver's door closed behind him and storms back to the cabin.

'What are you doing?' Kim asks her husband before he can get inside.

'I'm getting away before I say something I regret,' Lewis replies, and the glare he shoots Cole as he answers makes it clear who and what he is referring to. But maybe I should have the same sentiment. I should get out of here before I too say something I regret. The only problem is, there is no way of escaping any more.

'How are we going to go home?' I ask a little fearfully, terrified at the thought of having to be around Ryan, Kim and, by association, poor Cole, for a minute longer than I have to be.

'I don't know,' Lewis snaps back. 'I guess if we all start walking now then we could be back by Christmas.'

Sarcasm won't help matters but it's all Lewis has got before he disappears back inside.

'I'm sorry,' Cole says rather feebly then, clearly only having the confidence to speak once his father has left the scene.

Except of course, he hasn't left. Not really. He's standing there right next to him. If only Cole knew. But if I'm struggling to deal with the shock of it and I'm an adult, how is a teenager supposed to comprehend it all?

'How about we all go inside, have a cup of tea and make a plan?' Kim suggests in that good old-fashioned way of hoping that no matter what the problem may be, it's nothing that can't be made better by discussing it over a hot drink. War. Finances. Health. There's nothing that can't be put right, at least in the minds of the English, once a kettle has been boiled and a couple of cups taken out of the kitchen cupboard. But what about betrayal, infidelity and false parenthood? Can one teabag save all that or are we going to need something stronger?

A few specks of rain falling from the heavens above convince us that going back into the cabin is the best thing to do at present, so we all rather reluctantly head inside to where we know the angry Lewis is currently residing. We find him fiddling around with the Wi-Fi box in the lounge area when we walk in, and he's no doubt trying to re-establish an internet connection so he can either find an online tutorial on how to charge a dead car battery or at least find the contact details for the nearest mechanic who could come out and do it for us. I leave him to it as I go upstairs to check on Emily, wondering how she is getting on after having her own personal battles today.

She's curled up on her bed in the foetal position, her Harry Potter book in one hand while her other gently cradles her abdomen, and just like she has done for most of her life, she looks so delicate and precious to me in her vulnerable state.

'Hey, how's it going?' I say as I sit on the edge of her bed beside her and stroke a strand of her soft hair back from where it lies across her forehead.

'I'm okay,' Emily replies quietly. 'Why is Lewis shouting?'

'There's a problem with the car. But we'll fix it.'

Emily doesn't look like she cares to know too much more about the problem, nor does she ask me anything else about it. Instead, she just closes her book and seeks further reassurance that everything she has been through today is perfectly normal.

'Yes, of course it is,' I tell her again. 'There's nothing to worry about.'

But, of course, that is a lie and I know it even before I say it. That's because while I am worrying about the impact of Ryan's betrayal on my marriage, there is Emily to consider and how what her father has done will shape her life now going forward. She has a half-brother for one, something that will take some explaining and will undoubtedly cause her to question the solid family unit she once thought she was a part of. She will also see that her dad has deeply hurt her mum and that must have some kind of profound impact on her as well.

Will it affect her relationships with men when she is older? Will she be forever cursed with trust issues like I am cursed to be now? She doesn't deserve any of that. She's just a child, a happy, blossoming child. But her father's secrets and lies could shape the woman she eventually becomes far more than the years of hard work that have gone into raising her so far have already done, and that's just one more reason for me to hate Ryan and Kim.

'Do you want to come downstairs or stay up here for a little while?' I ask my, as yet, oblivious daughter, but she tells me she might have a little longer on her bed and I'm secretly pleased about that, as I'd rather she didn't have to deal with all of the drama that is going on down there.

I promise Emily I'll be back soon to check on her before I leave, and I have to take a very deep breath before returning to face everybody else again. When I do, I find that Lewis seems to have given up on getting the Wi-Fi working and now has another plan entirely.

'I'll have to walk to the main road and try and get a phone signal,' he says, and he looks like he means he is going now because he goes to pick his coat up from the back of the sofa.

'Don't be silly. How long will that take you?' Kim asks him.

'Hours, probably. But we don't have any other choice.'

'But it's raining out there.'

The weather has definitely worsened again, and the windows of the cabin are streaked with water once more.

'It's always raining,' Lewis mutters as he puts his coat on. 'If I wait for a sunny day around here then I'll be waiting a long time.'

'I think you should wait for the storm to pass.'

'I'd rather just get going. We need to call a mechanic and get them out to fix the car. God knows how long it will take them to get up here, but it needs to be done. Maybe I'll get lucky and catch a passing motorist out on the road and they might be able to help us. But staying here isn't going to do anything.'

'What's the rush? We're not due to leave for another forty-eight hours. Just go tomorrow. It's getting late now. You might not make it back before dark, and I don't think you should be wandering around out there when the light has faded.'

Kim's concern is valid. Based on the time of day and how far away the main road is, I doubt Lewis could make it there and back before the sun goes down. But he seems determined to try.

'Do you think I want to go out there? I'd much rather sit in the hot tub with another glass of wine. But I can't do that because somebody broke our car.'

Poor Cole is back in the firing line again and I look at the teenager in trouble, who is standing awkwardly in the kitchen listening to all of this, but now he just heads for the stairs, clearly not willing to stick around and be told off any more for his mistake.

'Yeah, that's right. You go back to your room and leave the adults to sort out your mess,' Lewis mutters, and I almost wish Kim would just let her husband leave because at least then he would give Cole a break.

'Let it go,' Ryan says suddenly. 'He's said sorry. Get off his back.'

'Sorry doesn't make it better,' Lewis replies quickly. 'Sorry isn't going to get us out of here now our car doesn't work.'

Cole slams his bedroom door above us before another loud noise fills the cabin. But that one came from outside. More thunder. Another storm. And only now does Lewis reconsider his plan to go outside into it.

'How about you go in the morning,' Kim says. 'I could make you some sandwiches. Pack you some proper supplies. It'll be more sensible than going now.'

Lewis doesn't say anything but that must be his way of admitting that Kim is right. Tomorrow will be better than today. A flash of lightning only confirms it even more.

Just like the sudden flash, I get an idea then and suggest it before I talk myself out of it.

'Ryan could go with you,' I say. 'Safer for two to go than just one.'

Ryan does not look like he is thrilled at that suggestion, nor does Lewis, but I've said it now and Kim agrees with me.

'That sounds like a good idea,' she says. 'Much safer than going alone.'

'I'll be fine by myself,' Lewis mumbles. 'No point in two of us losing our holiday.'

Ryan doesn't argue but I give him a nudge.

'No, it's okay, I don't mind,' he says, lying badly. 'I'll come with you. We'll be there and back in no time.'

With that seemingly agreed on, I feel pleased, or at least as pleased as I can be in the circumstances. That's because with the men out of the way tomorrow, I will have the time and space to speak to Kim about what I overheard her saying to Ryan, and when I do I will be expecting some answers. Much better to broach this awful subject with her than the men because I am fearful of how they will respond to it. I need to hear the truth for myself and make sure there are no misunderstandings before I do that and I'm going to get it from Kim. I just hope she can do me the decency of telling me everything. If she does, maybe I'll do her the decency of agreeing to not confront Ryan or tell Lewis what is going on until we have made it home, back to a more manageable environment.

I assume the men's trip to seek out help will be successful, but I guess we won't know until the morning. Until then, it's going to be a challenge to hold it all together.

It's going to be tough to stop everything falling apart.

FOURTEEN

NICOLA

The smell of barbecued meats fills the air as I step out onto the decking with a glass of wine in my hand. I told myself I wasn't going to drink tonight with all of this on my mind, but it quickly became apparent that I needed something to take the edge off my troubles. I'm not expecting to be able to get any sleep when I go to bed later, but at least I might be able to make it through the next couple of hours with some semblance of my mental clarity intact.

It was Kim's idea for us to have a barbecue, if only to keep us all busy, and it's certainly worked in the sense that it has kept all of us distracted after the dramas of this afternoon. Well, everybody that is except Lewis, who has not done too much recently other than sit in a camping chair on the edge of the decking and stare out into the abyss of rural Scotland. The fact he is so down about what has happened with the car makes me afraid of what he would be like if he knew what else was going on, but that's a problem for tomorrow and another gulp of my wine keeps that reminder at bay for the time being.

Unlike Lewis, I'm dealing with my problems by staying on the move, and after spending the last twenty minutes slicing up hot dog rolls and burger buns with Emily before we buttered them all and piled them high onto a large plate, I am now going to check out the current condition of the food on the barbecue. Ryan is standing in front of the grill, a pair of tongues in his left hand as he flips the meats in front of him to ensure they are being cooked evenly by the heat from the hot charcoals below. It looks like he has been doing a good job of it judging by how tasty the burgers and sausages look but he's not been working alone. Cole has been with him too and it's clear Ryan has been giving the teenager a tutorial on how to barbecue while they've been together.

I hang back a little from the pair and observe them for a moment, particularly interested in watching how Ryan interacts with Cole. I see that such an interaction is effortless for my husband as he confidently teaches his student about this particular method of cooking, no doubt operating under the knowledge that such an opportunity as this one is one of the few times he can ever pass on some wisdom to his son.

Unlike with Lewis, Cole is responsive and engaged with Ryan, and that's probably because Ryan is treating him like an adult rather than a child. He's not scolding the teenager or telling him to do something he doesn't want to do. He's just making things fun, giving some advice and, ultimately, allowing Cole to learn and develop in a relaxed way. In other words, he is being the perfect parent.

Except he's not, is he?

As much as what I know is tearing at my heart, I can't help but keep watching the pair with their backs turned to me and I'm thinking about how the son I was unable to give my husband has been provided to him by somebody else. Kim gave Ryan what he really wanted, and even though the situation is extremely complicated, my husband does have a boy of his own.

I remember that I came out here to check on the progress of the meal, so I'm just about to interrupt the male bonding time at the barbecue when I hear the sound of a bottle opening to my left. It's Lewis popping the top off another beer and when he sees me look over, he asks me if I'd like one.

He has the top off a second bottle before I can say no and then he taps on the empty camping chair beside him, inviting me to take a seat and give him some company.

I should just politely decline, check on the food and go back inside, but I feel so sorry for this man and the lies he has been told that I end his loneliness for a moment by easing myself into the chair.

'Cheers,' he says, clinking his bottle against mine. 'I was hoping that Cole might come and sit with me, but I guess he's having more fun over there.'

Cole's laughter drifts over from the barbecue amidst much sizzling and smoke and it's clear Cole is having a much better time there than he would here.

'You know what kids are like,' I say, trying to cheer him up. 'They're drawn to fire. I'm sure he'll sit with you after dinner.'

'I doubt it. I wouldn't want to if I was him. I was pretty hard on him after the car incident.'

'Maybe but he did something wrong, so you had to make that clear.'

'By being horrible to him?'

'I wouldn't say you were horrible to him.'

'I just couldn't stop. I saw red,' Lewis admits before tearing the corner of his bottle's label. 'I've been losing my temper more and more recently.'

While he hasn't offered an excuse as to why that is yet, nor does it excuse all the shouting, arguing and complaining he has done since we got here, it is good to at least hear that Lewis acknowledges he hasn't been the easiest person to be around this weekend.

'Can I tell you a secret?' Lewis asks me then, surprising me, and considering the secret that I am harbouring I worry about what he might say next.

'A secret?'

'Yeah.' His voice is low now, just loud enough for me to hear it but not enough for Ryan and Cole over by the barbecue.

He leans in a little closer to me until there's barely an inch between us and our camping chairs before he speaks again.

'I'm a little envious of your husband.'

'What? Why?'

Does he know about Cole's real father and Ryan sleeping with Kim? Has he somehow been living with that knowledge all this time and managed to pretend like he's fine with it? Am I really one of the last to know?

'He's just always so calm and in control,' Lewis says then. 'Doesn't get flustered like I do. Doesn't seem to have the weight of the world on his shoulders all the time, which must be a nice feeling because I can't relate to it. I mean, how can it be that a man who has less money, a fairly dull job and a modest home can be happier than me, a wealthy guy with my own business and a luxury holiday home?'

I realise then that Lewis doesn't know about the affair or Cole's real parentage and is instead just jealous of the fact that Ryan seems to be more at peace with his lot in life than he is.

'Well, there's more to life than money,' I remind Lewis, although such a comment seems a little strange to make as we're sitting on the decking of a lavish cabin in one of the most desirable parts of the UK while we wait for an array of expensive and tasty meats to finish cooking.

'I wish that was true,' Lewis replies, tearing an even bigger part of the label of his bottle.

'It is.'

'Try telling that to the bank who expects my mortgage payments on time. Or the guys at the tax office. Or my wife, who seems to be able to spend cash like it's going out of fashion.'

I detect a worrying tone to Lewis's voice and fear there might be something more going on with him than just a general sense of grumpiness about how today has gone.

'Are you having money troubles?' I ask, wondering if that could be it. 'Because if you are then it's okay. Nobody will judge you. But you need to tell Kim.'

'I'm fine.' The whole label comes off the bottle then. 'I'm just tired and not looking forward to a long walk to the main road tomorrow.'

I'm not looking forward to a long conversation with Kim tomorrow either, but it is what it is.

'Are you sure that's all it is?' I check one more time, but Lewis tosses the crumpled up label into the bin and nods his head.

'Yeah, don't worry about me. And I'd appreciate it if you could keep what I just said to yourself. The last thing I need is Ryan thinking I like him a lot more than I do.'

Lewis means that as a joke, but I don't laugh because, in a way, it was easier when I used to think that Lewis argued with my husband because he just disliked him. Now knowing that all the arguments mainly stemmed from Lewis wishing he was more like Ryan only makes me feel even worse about what I know.

'I thought you were going to report back on the food?'

Kim's voice brings an end to my quiet conversation with her husband, and I see her heading over to the barbecue with an empty plate in hand. When she gets there, she leans in beside Ryan and checks on the food before Cole tells her something and she smiles. I'm guessing he is telling her how much he has helped with the preparation of the meal and, for a moment, seeing the three of them standing together looking so happy, so at ease, makes me think about the family they could have been. But they are still a family of sorts, even if Lewis and I are in the way, and Emily's existence makes it more difficult. Ryan, Kim and Cole are bound together forever, whether all of them and anybody else knows it or not. Meanwhile, I feel like I'm sitting on the sidelines, much like Lewis is, and like the envy he feels towards Ryan I feel the same thing now towards Kim.

Of course, I could break up the perfect trio at the barbecue simply by standing up and saying what I overheard earlier. I doubt Kim and Ryan would be so relaxed then and it would give them a turn at being the bad guys instead of Lewis. But it's impossible. We're stuck in this place, miles from anywhere and with nothing but trees surrounding us. Lifting the lid on something so explosive in these circumstances would be even more devastating than usual.

As Kim takes the cooked pieces of meat from the barbecue, I head inside to join Emily at the table and, as dinner is served, we all grab our fair share of the hotdogs and burgers. Lewis's mood seems lifted somewhat by the meal because he lightens up a little, making a few jokes and suggesting more karaoke later, and that's good to see. The food has a slightly smaller impact on my own mood and despite forcing myself to eat something, all I really want to do is go and lie down in a dark room, curl up on a bed and cry. But I can't do that because such a thing would make it obvious that something is wrong, so I keep a brave face on things for a little while longer. At least I do until Emily starts being silly, playing with her food, not sitting still in her seat and, eventually, knocking over a glass of red wine that spills onto my meal and my lap.

'You clumsy girl!' I cry, jumping up from my seat and dabbing quickly at my stained jeans with a napkin. The volume of my voice stuns the room into silence, and everyone stares at me, shocked at the anger that just erupted from inside a person who is normally fairly quiet and reserved.

I know it was out of character for me, but I also know that these are not normal times, and despite apologising to Emily for shouting she leaves the table and runs upstairs.

'I'll go and see her,' Ryan offers, getting up from his seat, but I know it needs to be me who goes and not just because I'm the one who raised my voice at her and got her upset. It's also because I am on the verge of tears now and there's no way I can hold them back much longer.

'No, it's fine. I'll go!' I just about manage to croak out before rushing to the stairs and heading up as quickly as I can.

I can already feel my cheeks getting wet as I reach the landing and, once I'm out of view, I skip going into Emily's room and go straight into the bathroom instead. Then I lock the door, slump down to the ground and let my body do what it needs to do.

My eyes sting as the tears flow and I bury my mouth in the sleeve of my sweater to stifle my sobs.

It has happened. I've cracked. The shock of what I overheard has finally subsided and now the reality of the situation is hitting me.

So much for making it to tomorrow, when the mechanic is on his way and we have an escape route out of here, before I confront Kim.

At this rate, I doubt I can make it through the next hour.

FIFTEEN

NICOLA

Somehow, and I'm not exactly sure how, I was able to stem the flow of my tears and make it through until bedtime without blowing apart the peace in this cabin. But it wasn't easy, particularly when I watched Kim singing as part of a karaoke performance earlier and saw how much fun she was having. At least she enjoyed tonight because it will be the last night she will ever have of the rest of the world not knowing who she is and what she is capable of.

Ryan seemed to be enjoying himself as well, although he was a little more subdued than Kim, only singing one song to her four and mainly just relaxing on one of the sofas as the music played. Lewis did a song, as did Cole, but I declined, blaming tiredness for my inability to get up and perform for everybody. Little do they all know that I'm actually giving the biggest performance here and I'm continuing to give that performance as I get into bed now beside my husband.

I can tell he's had too much to drink because he's jabbering away incessantly, talking about all kinds of things like how we should book a family holiday abroad soon, even though money is tight, to how well he did with the barbecue and how he's always fancied doing some kind of cookery class because he really enjoys cooking when he actually has a go at it.

But I've barely been responding to his various comments and suggestions, more focused on getting settled under the duvet so I can turn the lights off and remove any chance of him seeing the tears that I expect will come again at some point during the night. At least Ryan will be asleep by then so he won't hear me crying, or at least I hope he will be. But as I reach out to turn off the bedside lamp, I feel Ryan's hands running over my legs.

'Leave the light for a minute,' he whispers to me with a stupid grin on his face. 'How about we have a little fun before we go to sleep...'

It's obvious what he's referring to but there's no way that's going to happen. I just need a good excuse as to why not.

'We can't. Someone might hear us,' I say, hoping that the thought of other people sleeping in rooms so close to our own might make him embarrassed enough to want to keep things quiet.

But it doesn't work.

'No one will hear us,' Ryan says, still grinning. 'Come on. We're on holiday. Let's enjoy ourselves.'

'I'm tired.'

'Then allow me to wake you up.'

'I don't know.'

'Come on.'

Now he's kissing my neck and I'm running out of time to stop him before he goes any further. Every kiss he gives me only makes me think of his lips on hers. Is this how he kissed Kim when they were together? Or did she seduce him? Did he need much persuading?

He's still trying to persuade me now but it's not long until the images of him in bed with my best friend are much too far at the forefront of my mind for me to do anything but push him away and make my point more sternly.

'I said no. I'm tired.'

Ryan isn't smiling any more and now just looks surprised. That quickly turns to him being grumpy with me and he huffs out a 'goodnight then' to me before rolling over and turning his back to me in the bed.

I don't have the energy or the inclination to apologise to him or explain why I couldn't bring myself to be intimate with him, and while I'm sure he's probably thinking it's because I'm not as much fun as I used to be, at least that stops him from figuring out the real reason, for the time being at least.

With the light off, I find a little comfort in the darkness and it's not long until I hear evidence that Ryan has fallen asleep, his heavy snoring the only sound now in this otherwise quiet cabin.

I lie there for what feels like an age listening to the breaths coming from my husband until I hear another sound. It's just outside the bedroom door and, as I listen, I detect footsteps passing by the room before they head downstairs.

I guess I'm not the only one who can't sleep.

But who else is having problems resting tonight?

I think about just staying in bed and leaving whoever it is to it, but I also worry that it might be Emily struggling to sleep after what happened to her earlier today, so I creep to the bedroom door and open it slightly before peering out in the hopes that I might get a look at who went downstairs.

Through a gap in the frame of the balcony, I can see the flickering light from the TV and that makes me even more worried that it is my daughter who has gotten up in the middle of the night, because I know the first thing she would do in such a situation would be to turn on the television. The volume is turned down low to not attract the attention of anybody upstairs but now I know somebody is down there, I leave my room and peer over the edge of the balcony. When I do, I see who it is that's sitting in front of the TV.

But it's not Emily.

It's Cole.

I see the teenager's face being illuminated by the glow from the screen and that's how I can register the troubled expression on his face. Never have I seen a youngster look so sad. Not even Emily has looked like Cole does right now. Something is on the boy's mind.

So I head downstairs to find out what it might be.

I make it halfway down the staircase before Cole realises someone is coming, and he grabs the remote control when he hears me, as if to turn off the TV quickly and make out like he was just about to go back to bed. But then he sees that's it me and not one of his parents and he relaxes a little. He relaxes even more when I tell him that I can't sleep either before I ask him what he's watching.

'I'm not sure what it is,' he admits. 'I think it's a reality show.'

'Ooh, my favourite,' I say as I take a seat beside him. 'I'm glad I got up now.'

I smile to let him know that he's not going to get in trouble for being out of bed, but he's so worried that he has to doublecheck for reassurance.

'You won't tell my parents, will you?'

'No, don't worry.'

I feel bad because he's clearly afraid of getting another telling off, but I think he's had more than enough lectures and admonishments for one day, so I won't be adding to his woes.

We watch the action on the screen for a few minutes in silence, although I use the term action loosely because it seems like not very much is happening at all in this particular TV show. Before I can ask Cole why he can't sleep tonight, he surprises me by asking me that very question first. Unfortunately, I can't be honest with him without giving him even more troubles, so I just say I never sleep well after a heavy meal and too much wine, and he accepts that because he has no reason not to.

'What about you?' I ask him. 'What's keeping you up?'

'Not much.'

'Oh, come on. I know that teenagers sleep for at least eighteen hours a day, if not more,' I joke. 'So there must be something wrong if you're not lying in your bed.'

Cole hesitates for a little while longer before admitting to me what it is.

'I feel like I can't do anything right. No matter what I do, I feel like my parents are always mad at me.'

'That's not true.'

'Yes, it is. Especially Dad. He's always having a go at me.'

I'm not sure what to say to that, but Cole carries on anyway.

'You've only seen what he's like this weekend, but I see it every day. He's always in a bad mood and he always takes it out on me. All he cares about is work but I think that's why he's always so angry. Now he wants me to go and do the same job as him when I leave school. But no thanks.'

Cole just admitting he has no desire to go and work in Lewis's business is not a huge surprise to me, but I wonder if he has shared that sentiment with anyone else before.

'Have you told your mum how you feel?' I ask, doing my best to gently steer the conversation away from Cole's father because, unbeknownst to the teen, that is not a straightforward topic any more.

'Yeah, last year I told her what I wanted to do,' Cole replies. 'I told her I wanted to go to college then university and study something to do with sports. Maybe sports science. I could be a physio for a football team. One of my friends' brothers does that and he says it's a cool job. He meets all the players and goes to all the matches.'

'What did your mum say when you told her that?'

'She just said I could do what I wanted to but that I had to be sure because Dad would be upset if I said no to working for him.'

'But the main thing is that you are happy. You know that, right?'

It feels weird to be trying to console someone else's child, although the fact is not lost on me that I'm far more closely connected to Cole than I thought when I woke up this morning. Technically, I'm his stepmother, although once I've had more time to process all of this and got the full story from Kim and Ryan about their fling, I'm not sure I'll be married to my husband for much longer.

It's also not lost on me that Cole has a strong interest in something that Ryan has shown a desire to do in the past. I remember when I met Ryan back in our twenties and he talked about the idea of wanting to work for a football team. He didn't express an interest in being a physio and was more looking to go down the administration or marketing route, but the same sentiment was there. He liked the idea of working for a big team, going to matches and being around the players. Exactly like Cole.

That was a dream that wasn't fulfilled for Ryan, even though I encouraged him to pursue it if that was what he really wanted to do, but Cole still has plenty of time to realise some of his ambitions. Or at least he does until he finds out that his whole life has been a lie.

There's no telling what route he will go down then.

'I just wish I could do what I wanted to do and didn't have Mum and Dad on my case all the time,' Cole admits, and I wish there was something I could say to make him feel better. Perhaps tell him that things will get easier, which would be true if not for the bombshell that would soon be coming his way. In the end, all I can do is remark on how late it is and how we should both try and get some sleep so we're not totally exhausted tomorrow, and he reluctantly agrees to go back to bed.

He turns the TV off and says goodnight and I smile as he heads up the stairs. But I don't follow him for a while, instead sitting in the dark downstairs for at least another hour. That's because I know that this will be the last night that things are relatively normal for that poor boy, just like they are for Emily who is hopefully already asleep.

Dawn is coming soon, and tomorrow is uncertain.

But one thing is definite.

By the time the sun sets tomorrow night, everything will be different.

Forever.

SIXTEEN

NICOLA

I eventually returned to my bed and lay down beside my husband for what might possibly be the last time. That's because once this 'holiday' is over then I doubt I'll ever be sharing a bed with Ryan again. That grim thought kept me occupied until the pale morning sunlight filtered through the curtains. When Ryan finally woke up and stretched his arms above his head, asking me how I'd slept, I was confident he had no idea I'd been tossing and turning all night long.

'Not bad,' I told him before disappearing into the bathroom to have a shower and put on some make-up to cover the heavy bags under my eyes.

By the time I come out, dressed and more prepared to face the day, Ryan is already downstairs with Emily and everyone else. They're tucking into tea and toast and running through the plan for today.

'We'll leave after breakfast,' Lewis says, mainly to Ryan, his companion on the upcoming trip. 'I figure we can cut through the forest and shave some time off the walk, so hopefully it'll only take about an hour and a half to get to the main road. But maybe we'll get lucky and pick up a phone signal before that.'

'Sounds good,' Ryan replies with a mouthful of toasted bread. 'I could use the exercise.'

'I think you both could,' Kim cuts in there as she watches her husband reach for another slice of toast.

'So what are you guys going to do while we're gone?' Ryan asks.

I can't answer that one without freaking him out, so I allow Kim to answer, not expecting her to have as much of a plan as Lewis does for his morning. But it turns out that she does.

'I thought we could make a picnic and go down to the loch seeing as how the weather has brightened up,' she says. 'Lunch by the loch, Emily. How does that sound?'

My daughter likes that idea and maintains her one hundred per cent record of never saying no to a picnic. But Cole isn't quite so thrilled.

'Boring,' he mutters.

'How about you come with us then?' Ryan suggests, inviting the teenager to join him and Lewis on their trek to the main road.

'A boys' trip. That's not a bad idea,' Kim replies, and I can't help but wonder if the pair have contrived to make what sounds like an innocent idea more about giving Ryan a little more time with his son.

'But it's miles,' Cole moans, not thrilled about the prospect of walking for hours any more than he is about going for a picnic.

'It'll be fun,' Ryan says cheerily. 'We can take some supplies, talk about football and action films and our celebrity crushes and whatever else we can't talk about in front of women. Isn't that right, Lewis?'

Lewis can't argue with that, although I'm sure Cole would appreciate it if his dad was a little more excited about the prospect of him joining them on the walk.

'The boys have the morning together and the girls can do

the same,' Kim says, confirming the idea. 'Sounds good to me. What do you think, Nic?'

I think that I don't really care as long as I get five minutes alone with Kim to ask her if she really has slept with my husband and stabbed me in the back, so I just shrug and say why not.

'Let's see what supplies we can find in the fridge for our expedition,' Lewis says, getting up and going into the kitchen.

'An expedition? That's a very impressive way of describing a short walk,' Kim retorts with a laugh.

'A short walk? We're going miles, I'll have you know,' Ryan chimes in. 'Over treacherous landscape and doing battle with who knows what out there in the forest. Some of us might not make it back alive.'

'Oh, really, it's that dangerous, is it?'

'It sure is. I'd say we're very brave for undertaking such a journey.'

Ryan and Kim seem to be enjoying their light-hearted banter, or is it flirting? I don't know but I don't like Ryan's last comment. *Some of us might not make it back alive.* I know he was only joking so why did my stomach lurch when he said it? Is it because I'm aware that today is D-Day for the truth to come out? Is his jesting actually an ominous warning?

Lewis is putting numerous things from the fridge into a backpack, clearly looking forward to the trip with Cole, and as Ryan and the teenager get themselves ready to leave, I tell Emily to go and prepare for the picnic.

By the time the boys are standing by the door with their coats and boots on and one full backpack full of supplies to share between them, I get the feeling that I should stop this. Say something now before they have chance to leave. Do it while everyone is here instead of waiting until we have all split up. It only takes one look at the useless car outside to remind me that it will be better to wait. Saying something now will not change the fact that somebody is going to have to walk to the main road and make an emergency phone call, and it's surely far easier for them to do that now than after they hear what I have to say. So I stay quiet as the three males say their goodbyes to us.

Ryan gives me a hug and a kiss before doing the same to Emily, and she tells him that she will miss him. It's another reminder that things are going to be so difficult when everything comes out and Ryan and I separate, forcing our daughter to have to split her time between us. But I can only do what is best for me at the moment because while my daughter will have the chance to one day find herself a man who might love her, I cannot stomach one more day potentially being with a man who does not love me.

'We'll be back before you know it,' Lewis says as he waves goodbye.

'Enjoy the picnic,' Ryan calls as he follows.

'Bye Mum,' Cole mumbles as he brings up the rear and the three of us in the doorway of the cabin watch them depart.

Kim is waving them off, as is Emily. But I'm not moving. I'm just staring at my husband and wondering what he will say to me the next time he sees me. He'll be apologising, I guess, because he'll come back to find Kim in tears after I've exposed them both. The main thing is that there will be a mechanic coming behind them to fix the car so we can leave here.

I hope it doesn't take them too long to find a phone signal.

And I hope it takes even less time for Kim to tell me the truth at the picnic.

SEVENTEEN

RYAN

There is something to be said for the calming effects of being out in nature. Getting away from all the things in life that stress us out so much. People. Buildings. Traffic. Noise. Pollution. It's freeing and, most of all, it's a reminder that not everything has to wear us down. Some things can recharge us too. Like the abundance of fresh air filling my lungs as I step over fallen logs in this forest and slip through gaps in the trees. Like the sight of the three deer grazing peacefully nearby, a small family living out here in the wild with no need for anything but food, water and each other. And most of all, the unrelenting quietness, a quietness so strong and soothing that it almost feels like it's massaging my mind as I move deeper into it, as well as making me wonder why my ancestors ever chose to abandon inhabiting areas like this in favour of areas full of concrete and cars.

Like the trio of deer spotted earlier, I'm part of a trio myself, although it's one that is much less at home in this unfamiliar landscape as those other mammals. Lewis is in front of me, striding ahead in his eagerness to reach the main road, but occasionally stumbling in his haste and being forced to slow down unless he wants to add a sprained ankle to his list of grievances this weekend.

I'm in the middle of the pack, the rucksack full of snacks on my back, and I'm taking a little more time to negotiate the foliage all around us because I'm not as desperate as Lewis to get out of here. That's because I'm enjoying one of the few times of the year that I actually get to spend quality time with my secret son.

It's my son who completes the trio, and Cole is walking behind me and at the slowest pace of all, a teenager who hates spending time with his parents anywhere, let alone in the middle of nowhere. Except he is under the false belief that it is the man two places ahead of him that is his father and not the man directly in front. Maybe things would be different if he knew the truth. Maybe he would be happier to spend time with me than he is with Lewis. Maybe I'd be happier too because I would be able to get closer to Cole naturally and not have to act out this charade for a minute longer than I have already done.

'Favourite TV show?' I ask my travel companions, suggesting another topic for discussion after I have already had us discuss films and music, running through topics as quickly as I can because it won't be long before Cole is absent from my life again, once we return home.

'I don't really watch TV anymore,' Cole admits. 'I prefer playing video games now.'

'That's an understatement,' Lewis adds but that's all he seems to want to say on the matter.

Cole's admission that he prefers video gaming to watching TV these days is another reminder of how I am always playing catch-up when it comes to knowing about what is going on in his life. The only times I get to be around him are when Nicola and Kim arrange a get-together of our two families and I can be in Cole's presence. It's during those times that I try to glean as much information as I can about my boy without arousing any suspicions. Of course, I've always had the option of pressing Kim for facts but she made it clear that it would be risky to do so. The fewer phone calls and messages between us the better, and I get that, not that it makes it any easier. On the other hand, I realised early on that the more I know about Cole, the harder it is for me to handle not being closer to him, so there have been times when I have gladly accepted being on the periphery of his life, if only to spare the heartache that comes from knowing just how much I am actually missing out on.

'Fair enough,' I say in response to Cole's admission regarding his leisure time preferences these days. 'I played a lot of video games when I was your age too, although they weren't as good as they are now,' I say, mainly talking to Cole rather than Lewis, as I have been doing for most of this hike. 'You should see the graphics back then, not that we knew how bad they were at the time. We were just happy to have a game to play.'

'I play online mostly, so I can talk to my friends at the same time.'

'That's another thing we didn't have. When we played, it was just against the computer, not a real person.'

Cole and I spend the next ten minutes discussing the differences between video games then and now and I feel like we're both enjoying the comparison. Most of all, I feel like Cole is enjoying having somebody show an interest in one of his hobbies, and it strikes me how easy it can be to be a good parent.

Just be interested in what your kids do.

Unfortunately, it also helps if that kid knows exactly who their real father is.

As I have done for much of the last fifteen years, I wish there was some way that Cole could know the truth without it blowing up all of our lives. Of course I regret my brief fling with Kim because I love Nicola and never meant to hurt her, but I can't say I regret the result of it. A little boy. My dream. But it became a dream that has slowly turned into a nightmare.

The affair with my partner's best friend was not premeditated, rather the result of just sheer destiny and happenstance, or at least that's what I've always told myself. Having known Kim for almost as long as I'd known Nicola, considering how the two friends were joined at the hip, I'd found her to be friendly, funny and fairly attractive, although the idea of taking anything further with her had never really crossed my mind. Not until a house party in which Nicola got stupidly drunk, picked a fight with me over what turned out to be a simple misunderstanding and then left me behind to go to another party with some other friends. I had no idea she had gone until Kim told me, when she mentioned that my new wife had left with a group including a couple of guys. I guess I got jealous and suspected she had had enough of me and felt like having a little fun with somebody else.

We were in our early twenties and not the mature, more sensible versions of ourselves that we are now. I guess that's why I made the decision that night to focus less on Nicola and more on Kim, the friend who had always been nothing but nice to me. I knew she was in a relationship of her own at the time, a guy called Lewis who I had never really got on with particularly well because he was always talking about how much his car and clothes cost, and how he was so much better off financially having his own business than all the poor students who had left university with so much debt. I had experienced what it was like to be a poor student myself and was still poor despite graduating and entering the working world at the time, so I'd resented him and his cockiness. I guess that was why I didn't care so much about him when Kim told me she wasn't particularly happy in her relationship.

I confessed to feeling the same with Nicola and the next thing we knew, the pair of us were kissing. Only it went much further than that and, before we knew it, we had ended up in bed together in one of the upstairs rooms at the party. But nobody ever caught us, just like nobody found out what we did even to this day.

The day after it happened, I'd wondered if perhaps it should be Kim and I who were together and that leaving our respective partners might be the best thing all around. But that notion was squashed by a couple of things that happened that day. Firstly, Kim told me it had been a mistake and she was happier with Lewis than she had made out after all. I suspected her happiness stemmed more from the money he had than anything else but, regardless of that, she told me she wanted to stay with him and urged me to keep what had happened between us quiet. And secondly, Nicola apologised to me for how she had behaved at the party, making it clear that she had only left with those other guys to make me jealous, which was obviously childish, but we were young and nobody's perfect then, are they?

With what happened with Kim apparently just a one-time thing, and with Nicola making it clear she really did want to be with me, I foolishly figured everything could just go on as it had before that night. That was until I found out Kim was pregnant and, even though she said nothing to suggest anybody but Lewis was the father, I knew the date of conception must have been very close to the time we slept together. So I confronted her immediately and asked her for the truth. Told her to tell me if the baby was mine or not. She insisted it wasn't and begged me to keep my theory to myself. But I couldn't and threatened her with a paternity test once the baby arrived.

And that was when she admitted the truth...

I look over my shoulder now at the boy walking behind, a boy who has grown from a small child and will soon be a man. But it's a development that I have only been on the outskirts of. I haven't been witness to all of it, like a real father should be.

Not like with Emily. I have been there every step of the way through all the stages of my daughter growing up. I have missed so much with Cole, only seeing him once every few weeks at best when the two families meet up, although sometimes it's ended up being months if Nicola's and Kim's calendars haven't aligned. I guess that's the price I have had to pay for what I did.

But considering I don't like it, what's stopping me from telling the truth?

Besides the fact that I know Nicola would leave me instantly and take Emily with her, I also know that I would turn Cole's world upside down and make him doubt everything he has ever been told in his short life. It would be a cruel thing to do, even if it would be the honest thing. And then there's the small matter of how Lewis would take it. If I had to guess, I'd say he would stop at nothing short of killing me and could I really blame him?

Perhaps the only thing weirder than walking ahead of a boy who is secretly my son is walking behind a man who would murder me if he knew what I'd really done.

So much for finding peace out in nature.

Even here, I'm still in a world of pain.

There was a time when I thought about ending things with Nicola, aware that it might alleviate some of the guilt I continually felt about what I'd done behind her back. I realised that such a drastic measure would have only left me even worse off than I was. I'd likely lose much of my access to Emily as a result, because I'm sure Nicola would claim full custody of her. While I might be able to reveal the truth about Cole, I'd still only see him sparingly because I'd be unlikely to get custody over his own mother. At least staying with Nicola meant I was always in Kim's orbit and, by extension, Cole's. Being a part of two dysfunctional families had to be better than being all by myself, cut adrift from the two children I had fathered and the two women I had been involved with.

Either way, it was a pretty bleak decision to have to make.

The trees are so tall in this part of the forest that they are mostly blocking out the sunlight, leaving us to walk in a gloomy, pale hue, one that makes this place look and feel even more mysterious than it already does. But it's one of those tall trees that attracts the attention of Cole, and he suddenly veers off from the line we were cutting through the foliage and heads over to the base of one of the trunks. Then he starts climbing surprising quickly, showing an adeptness at scaling the various limbs that protrude from the tall tree.

'Come on, Cole, we don't have time for this,' Lewis grumbles as we watch the teenager ascending, but I shrug and suggest he might be able to see how far the main road is from up there if he can get high enough. But I am also a little worried that he might go too high and end up falling, so I'm relieved when I see him stop on a branch halfway up the tree and just sit for a moment.

'How's the view up there?' I ask him, and he gives me a thumbs up, a gesture that I appreciate and savour because while it's only a small thing, it means a lot to see my son happy.

'He's always been climbing trees,' Lewis tells me as we stand below and look up. 'I thought he'd grow out of it, but I guess not.'

'It's nice that he hasn't,' I reply. 'Shows there's still a little child in there somewhere even though he's getting older.'

That glimpse of the child Cole used to be only makes my heart ache even more for what I've missed out on seeing with my own eyes. But before I can feel too sorry for myself, Lewis speaks again and when he does, it's in the form of a confession. It's a rather unusual and unexpected confession and one that leads to me seeing him in a very different light.

Little do I know it, but it's not the only confession going on in the area at the same time.

EIGHTEEN

NICOLA

This is certainly a scenic spot for a picnic, on the banks of a loch that is surrounded on all sides by lush greenery and beneath a blue sky that is totally unspoilt by clouds, a sight that has long been wished for since I got here.

On any other day, I'd be taking photos and thinking about how lucky I am to be here.

But today I'm not here to enjoy the view, nor could I even if I wanted to with so much on my mind.

Kim and I are seated on a large tartan picnic blanket beside a hamper full of snacks and champagne, while Emily is sitting on the grass a little way ahead of us, reading her book. It was my suggestion for her to go and do that, telling her to read a couple of chapters before we eat so she can tell me all about what is happening in her story. It's a good way to encourage her to read, but today it's a good way of getting her out of the way so I can ask Kim if she has really been lying to me throughout most of our friendship.

'How nice is it with the men not around?' Kim asks me, leaning back on her elbows and stretching out her long legs on the blanket. 'Far less tension when it's just the girls, right? I guess it's all that testosterone. I have to say, I envy you a little for having a daughter. I imagine they're easier than boys.'

'Maybe, but us females can be difficult too,' I reply, aware of how big an understatement that will prove to be over the next few minutes. And now it's enough of the chit-chat.

It's time to ramp this thing up.

'How long have we been best friends for?' I ask Kim, even though I obviously know the answer. But I want it to be at the forefront of her mind as I get to my point.

'Oh, it's been a long time,' comes the casual reply.

'It has, hasn't it? All that time being so close to each other. Telling each other everything. Having no secrets.'

I keep my eyes on Kim, but she is just savouring the view and doesn't appear fazed by what I've just said.

'That's true, isn't it?' I ask. 'There aren't any secrets between us, are there?'

'Nope.'

Another calm reply. Kim's as cool as the water in the loch.

'You'd tell me if there was, right?'

'What do you mean?'

'If there was something you were keeping from me. You would tell me eventually, wouldn't you?'

Only now does Kim look at me and it's possibly the first time she is getting the hint that something might be wrong.

'What are you talking about?'

'I'm talking about us being best friends. We still are, aren't we?'

'Of course we are! Don't be silly.'

Kim laughs and reaches into the hamper to take out the bottle of champagne. But before she can, I put my hand on her arm to tell her that's not what I'm here for.

'Then why have you been lying to me?'

Kim freezes, her skin as icy as I imagine this part of the world is in winter.

'W-w-what?' she stammers.

'I asked you why you been lying to me.'

Now I'm the calm one, at least on the surface anyway. But inside, my heart is beating faster than that woodpecker is hammering into that tree in the background.

'I don't know what you mean.'

Kim has removed her hand from the champagne bottle now, so I take my own hand from her arm. But that doesn't mean I'm easing off on her. Not one bit.

'I overheard you and Ryan talking in the hot tub,' I say, trying to stop my own voice from shaking now because saying out loud the thing I have been wrestling with for the last twenty-four hours is not easy.

'What? When?'

'Yesterday. I was in the bathroom above you and the window was open. And I heard what you were talking about.'

I have to pause for a moment to compose myself before I get to the main point. And then I force myself to say it.

'I heard Ryan say that Cole was his.'

Kim's eyes go wide with shock then but it's not the shock of somebody having heard something so ridiculous that they can't comprehend it. Rather, it's the shock of somebody who has just been caught out.

'Is it true?' I ask, tears now filling my eyes. 'Is Ryan Cole's dad? Did you sleep with him? Did you two have an affair?'

'Nic, wait. I—'

'Just tell me the truth. Please!'

I fear for a moment that Emily might have just heard my desperate plea from thirty yards away, but she hasn't because she is still facing the loch with her head buried in her book.

'We can't do this here,' Kim tells me, and she goes to get up, but I grab her arm again and this time I don't let go.

'Tell me the truth,' I urge her, desperate, afraid but also willing to suffer so long as I know what is really going on.

Kim glances at Emily but I tell her not to worry about her. And only then does my best friend reveal to me who she really is.

'I'm so sorry,' she begins, probably hoping that will take the sting out of what comes next.

'So it's true?'

Kim hesitates before nodding her head.

I grit my teeth and I have to wait a moment for the urge to slap her across the face to pass. That's just one of the many acts of violence I consider committing against the lying, cheating woman sitting next to me on this blanket and it's not easy to show restraint after being told the awful truth. The fact I manage it is an achievement and I suspect it's Emily's presence here that has prevented me from erupting so violently.

'What happened?'

'It was nothing. Just a one-time thing.'

'So, you slept with Ryan? When, exactly?'

'It was after a party. You two had had a fight and you'd left early with some other friends. Ryan was upset because he thought you were chasing some other guy. I told him you weren't, but it was clear he wasn't happy.'

'I remember that night. We were married then!'

'I'm sorry. It just happened.'

'How the hell did it just happen?'

'I ended up telling him that I was having a few problems with Lewis too and the next thing we knew, we were kissing. We were both drunk, that's the only reason it happened, I swear!'

'So what? You just had sex and thought nothing more of it? No harm done, as it were?'

'No, of course not! I felt terrible! We both did.'

'How could you do that to me? We were best friends!'

'I don't know! It was an accident. We were young. Stupid. Drunk!'

'Stop blaming it on alcohol. That's no excuse!'

I notice Emily turn her head then, but I give her a quick wave to let her know that everything is all right, and she goes back to her book. But it's a good reminder for me to try and keep my voice down.

'And Cole? He was the result of this one-night stand?'

Kim nods her head, her face paler than I thought possible.

'Are you being honest with me? You expect me to believe this only happened once?'

'I swear. It was a one-off!'

I study Kim's face for the truth, but what gives me the confidence to think I can spot a lie now after being fooled for so long by this woman? But she is adamant it only happened once, although I'm not sure that makes me feel too relieved. I guess it's better than a drawn-out affair, but it's still utterly devastating.

'And he's definitely not Lewis's? You know that for a fact?'

'Yes. I hoped he was, but I had a test done and Ryan is the father.'

I can't hide the disgust on my face at the thought of Kim secretly waiting for the results of a paternity test while Lewis happily carried on with life thinking he was the father of the baby in his home.

'How could you not tell Lewis? How could you not tell me?'

'I couldn't! It would break his heart. And I didn't want to lose him. I didn't want to lose either of you.'

'You should have thought about that before you slept with Ryan.'

'I know and I'm sorry. I'm so, so sorry.'

'So what happened? How did Ryan find out?'

'He suspected straight away. I guess he knew the dates matched.'

I shake my head in disgust again.

'And then he threatened to tell you and Lewis what we had done. So I did what I had to do to spare you both the pain. I told Ryan that as long as he kept our secret safe, I would let him see Cole as much as possible. If not then I would take him away and he'd never see him.'

'How did you do that?'

'Me and you see each other all the time so I knew it would be easy to keep them close. I'd come to visit you when I knew Ryan would be in too and I'd bring Cole so he could see him. Then there's things like this. Weekends away together.'

'You're telling me all your visits and all our holidays together as families have secretly just been about giving Ryan the chance to see Cole?'

This just gets worse and worse. I can't believe the depths that the pair of them have gone to in order to keep this charade going. All the times Cole was a baby and Kim would visit with him, handing the small child to me before inviting Ryan to have a hold. There I was thinking my partner was nervous and reluctant to have a newborn in his hands yet, in reality, he was happy because he was holding his son.

I need to get off this blanket and get out of here and I need to do it fast because I'm going to be sick.

I leap up and start grabbing a few of my things but Kim tries to stop me before I can go.

'What are you going to do?' she begs to know. 'Nic! Please, just wait a minute and let's talk about this.'

'I don't want to talk about it!' I snap back, pure hatred for this woman emanating from every pore of me. 'And I don't want to be around you for a minute longer than I have to be. As soon as that car is fixed and we're out of here then I never want to see you again.'

'Nic, wait! You don't mean that!'

'Yes, I do!'

I can't help shouting so loudly and Emily definitely heard

that, closing her book and standing up and looking back at the pair of us on the picnic blanket with concern in her eyes. But I'm not bothered about keeping quiet now, so I beckon my daughter over to join me.

'Come on, Emily, we're going!'

'What about the picnic?'

'We're not having a picnic. Not today.'

'But Mum.'

Emily's whining is the last thing I need so I make my wishes even clearer.

'Emily! Get here now!'

I don't think I've ever raised my voice quite so loudly to my daughter and the sight of her flinching proves it. But she does as I say and sheepishly walks over to me before I grab her hand and pull her away from the serene setting we were once enjoying.

'Nic! Wait! You can't tell Cole or Lewis! Please, it would destroy them!'

I ignore Kim and keep rushing away, though Emily is slowing me down considerably.

'What is she talking about, Mummy?' she asks me, looking back at Kim who is desperately scooping up the picnic stuff as she prepares to leave as well.

'Nothing! Just hurry up!' I say, eager to get back to the cabin and get packed up so we're ready to go when the men return and tell us the mechanic is on the way to fix the car.

'Nic! Please!'

Kim's cries continue behind me but I rush into the trees and lead Emily as quickly as I can through the forest, while I give no chance for the bitch behind me to catch up.

It's only right that she is terrified of what I might say to Cole and Lewis, but at the moment my only priority is getting myself and Emily back home. There'll be plenty of time for recriminations afterwards. All I needed to know was the truth and now that I have it, I can leave this place behind and try to salvage whatever future I have left. But who cares about Kim's future? Not me.

She can rot out here for all I care.

Just like Ryan can.

NINETEEN

RYAN

I'm still looking at Cole up in the tree high above us but I'm also listening to what Lewis is saying beside me. And it's not what I expected to hear.

'You're so much better with him than me,' Lewis begins, and it takes me a moment to realise he is referring to Cole.

'What?'

'You've got such an easy way with him. It looks effortless. But it always feels like such hard work for me.'

'What are you talking about?'

Lewis lets out a deep sigh then, the kind a man makes when he's finally releasing something that he's been bottling up for a while.

'He likes you. Respects you. I'm not sure he feels the same way about me.'

'Lewis, I—'

'Why do you think I'm so argumentative with you? It's because I'm jealous. It's childish, I know, but it's the way it is. I should be happy with everything I've got but I'm not and a big reason for that is I feel like I'm a rubbish dad.'

'Don't be stupid. You're a great dad,' I say, scarcely believing that I'm in a position where I'm having to convince the person who is not my son's real father how good of a parent he is to him.

'I don't know. Am I? Then why does Cole react so badly to everything I say? Why does he not talk to me like he does with you? Why can't I make him laugh or smile?'

'All kids argue with their parents. It's part of the job. It's only natural that they get along better with people who aren't giving them orders and telling them what they can't do.'

This might be the most awkward conversation that I've ever had, and I want it to end quickly. But I have a feeling that it won't as long as Cole is out of earshot up in that tree because Lewis is clearly taking this chance to get some things off his chest. And it doesn't end there. He has something else he wants to tell me.

'There's another reason I've been so uptight this weekend,' he says, his head bowed and his eyes on the soil by our feet, suggesting he is ashamed of what he is about to say. 'My business isn't going as well as I've been making out. I'm losing money, not making it and I'm trying everything but I'm not sure how I'm going to turn it around.'

That's a shocking revelation considering all the times before when Lewis has so openly flaunted his wealth in front of me. From cars to holidays to the spectacular cabin in this forest that he is hosting me in this weekend, he has never been shy in telling me how rich and successful he is. Yet now he's admitting that it's all a façade.

'What? How long have you been struggling?' I ask him.

'Last year was hard but I managed to keep afloat,' he admits. 'This year has been even worse and I'm not sure how much longer I can keep it quiet from everyone. I've got employees, clients, all sorts of people who depend on me. And that's before Kim and Cole.'

'Have you told Kim about this?' I ask though I have a feeling

I might already know the answer based on how happy she has been this weekend. She hasn't displayed any signs of worrying about money, not with all the champagne she bought and her excessive use of the hot tub that I imagine is accompanied by a fairly hefty energy bill.

'No, how can I?' Lewis moans. 'She'd leave me.'

'No, she wouldn't.'

'Yes, she would,' Lewis says, finally bringing himself to look at me now and I can see he genuinely believes what he is saying. 'She isn't in love with me. She's in love with the lifestyle I give her. But she'll soon get bored when all that goes away.'

'Is it that bad?'

'Yeah.'

'Can't you just sell a few things?'

'Like the cabin? Yeah, but we'd lose money on it with the economy like it is at the moment. I didn't even want to buy the damn thing, but Kim talked me into it. Said it would be the perfect place for us to take friends. Really what she meant is it's the perfect place to show off to our friends. Friends like you and Nicola, I suppose.'

It really sounds like Lewis is in a hell of a mess, but it also sounds like I never really knew this guy at all. All this time I've thought he was just nothing more than a flash, arrogant businessman and it turns out half of the 'showy' things he has done are down to his wife's influence rather than his.

'I don't know what to say,' I mutter, being honest. 'I'm sorry.'

Lewis shrugs and looks back to Cole who has now started descending the tree.

'Is there anything I can do to help?' I ask, although Lewis must know I don't have much money of my own to offer him.

'Just keep this to yourself?' Lewis asks me. 'Don't tell Kim. I mean, I'll tell her soon but I'm not ready yet. I just needed somebody to get it off my chest to. I guess you were the unlucky sod who drew the short straw there.'

He laughs at his sorry state of affairs before looking up and watching as Cole leaps down from the lowest branch and lands back on the forest floor beside us.

'Good fun?' Lewis asks, and Cole shrugs and says it was all right.

'Did you see the main road from up there?' I ask him, but Cole just shakes his head and says there were too many trees around. Then we all set off again, rested from our short break, or at least physically anyway. But mentally, that was an exhausting stop-off, because now I know that Lewis is struggling internally not only with his relationship with Cole but also his business that provides his family's only source of income, and I'm worried for him. I also feel a hundred times worse about the secret I have been keeping from him.

I'm worried for Cole now too because if Lewis is in financial difficulty and ends up losing his business, what state will that leave them all in? Will they lose their home? Move elsewhere? Will I see Cole less then? What about Cole's schooling? Not only is it an important time in his education but he attends a private school, and they are never cheap. Will he be kicked out if the fees can't be paid? Could he find another school to sit his final exams? If not, such a thing might destroy his career prospects going forward. Even at a granular level I'm worried at the thought of my boy going hungry if his 'father' is no longer able to provide for him. He's made me promise not to tell Kim, but how can I not when it affects our son?

I have plenty to keep my mind occupied as we walk on, but Lewis is doing a good job of disguising his woes by trying to make conversation with Cole about music. He's asking about bands he'd like to see in the future and Cole is giving plenty of answers, not that Lewis knows too much about the artists that are being mentioned. But I do because I have made the effort to listen to the music my son likes as it's one way of making me feel closer to him, although just like Lewis, I do my own job of disguising the truth by not revealing it. Instead, I begin to ponder one important question that weighs heavier on my mind the further I walk into this forest and that is: why did Lewis tell me about his problems? I know he said he needed somebody to get it off his chest to but there must be a hundred people he could have thought of before he landed on me. Then again, maybe he doesn't have that many friends, or maybe there's something about being out here in this unique environment that compelled him to get it off his chest with the guy accompanying him on this walk.

Whatever the reason, I wish he hadn't told me because it's given me even more to worry about. In fact, finding the main road and getting a phone signal is now the least of my problems, although it is still an issue that needs resolving. Fortunately, half an hour later, we make it to the main road and five minutes after that, Lewis declares that he has picked up a signal on his phone.

After using his data to search for the nearest vehicle recovery service in the area, he makes the call while Cole and I stand by on the side of the road, out of the way of any traffic that might pass by here. But the road is quiet, and we see no cars as we wait for Lewis to rejoin us.

While we are waiting, I take the opportunity to have some much-treasured private time with my son and ask Cole if he is enjoying himself on this weekend.

'It's all right,' he mumbles as he tries to find a signal on his own phone. He seems very eager to get one, which makes me think he is either missing having a connection to the internet or he is missing somebody in the real world.

'So, what's their name?' I ask him, guessing that there might be a special someone in his life that is on his mind now.

'What?'

'Whoever it is you're so desperate to text. What's their name?'

'How do you know there's someone?'

'Because I was fifteen once and there's always someone.'

Cole knows I have him beat there but he's still being coy.

'I'm not telling you.'

'Because you think I'll tell Lewis? Don't worry, I won't.'

Cole thinks about it for a moment before still refusing to give me an answer.

'Okay, fine. You won't tell me their name. What about how you know them? Are they in your school.'

Cole nods.

'Do they know you like them?'

'Yeah, I think so.'

'That's a good start. I was terrible at telling girls that I liked them when I was your age. I guess you're better at it than I am.'

'Did you have many girlfriends? Before Nicola?'

'I had a few. What about you? Is this person the one for you or do you like to play the field?'

'What does that mean?'

I laugh. 'Never mind.'

I can see that Cole is still frustrated at not being able to get a signal of his own and I imagine he is very stressed about what might happen if he doesn't contact the girl he likes. Paranoia is a real problem at the best of times but especially in the teenage years, so with that in mind, I try to offer a little parental wisdom in the guise of just a little advice coming from a family friend.

'Don't worry, if she really likes you, she won't care if you text her or not,' I say. 'And try not to worry if things don't work out with this one. It might not seem like it now but there will be plenty more chances. You've got your whole life ahead of you and, for that, I envy you.'

Cole thinks about what I've just said, or at least I hope he does and isn't just daydreaming about something else. It's hard to tell with him. But I do hope I might have been able to make him see things a little differently and that's all I can do for him, which will have to be enough.

Lewis ends his call then and walks back over to us, and I'm grateful for my little insight into how my son's love life is going, particularly because I imagine Lewis knows nothing about the girl at Cole's school that has him so enamoured.

'What did they say? Are they sending somebody out?' I ask Lewis.

'Yeah, they said they know where we are. But it'll be a few hours before they reach us.'

'I guess we might as well head back and kill one or two of those hours then,' I say and turn to go. But before I can, Lewis suggests we make the journey back a little more interesting and unzips his backpack before revealing a small bottle of whiskey.

'Who fancies a drink?' he asks but he isn't just looking at me. He's asking Cole as well.

'Are you serious?' the teenager asks, no longer bothered about trying to find a phone signal now that alcohol is being offered to him.

'Yeah, why not? Let's have a little fun. I'm sure the girls are having plenty without us.'

TWENTY

NICOLA

Emily has not been happy with me ever since I cut short the picnic and told her we were going back to the cabin. She's even unhappier when we make it back there and I tell her to go to her room and start packing her things.

'Why?' she whines, stamping her feet too for good measure.

'Just do as I say,' I tell her, not in the mood for any games. But before she can go to her room, I need Kim to unlock the door to this cabin to let us in. As she catches up to us, I ask her for the key.

'No, not until we've talked this through,' she replies in response.

'Not in front of Emily,' I say as my little girl stops stamping and watches us, sensing the atmosphere has turned sour again.

'Fine, I'll open the door but then you're going to listen to me.'

Kim steps past us and puts the key in the lock, and as soon as the door is open I guide Emily inside. But she is dragging her feet and it's because she wants to know what is going on between me and Kim.

'It's just adult stuff,' I say before telling Emily to go upstairs again. I'm relieved when she listens to me, but not thrilled about the fact that she stamps her feet loudly on every single step on the way up. It's not easy when my daughter is behaving like this and especially not when I know she has done nothing wrong. Her tantrum has only been caused by me unexpectedly changing the plans and cutting our holiday short and not by anything she has done, which makes me feel bad for having to ruin her fun.

The only person in the wrong here is the woman standing behind me.

And it's not long before she tries apologising again.

'I'm so sorry,' Kim says, her voice quaking with emotion. 'I don't want this to come between us.'

'Oh, that's very big of you,' I snarl back. 'You don't want you sleeping with Ryan to come between us. How about I sleep with Lewis, and we'll see how you feel then?'

Nothing like a bit of sarcasm to soothe the soul.

'Come on, Nic, don't be like that. I'm saying sorry. What more can I do?'

'How about just leave me alone before I hit you.'

Kim looks shocked that I would even suggest such a thing, but I mean it. If she takes one more step towards me then I won't be held responsible for my actions.

Rather wisely, she keeps her distance and just takes a seat on one of the sofas instead. I check my watch then and try to figure out how long the guys have been gone and when they might return. But, even in the best-case scenario, it's going to be a while and that's before whatever mechanic gets out here to look at the car. So I'm stuck here for now and Kim knows it.

'What are you going to do when they get back?' she asks me as I adjust one of the curtains so I can get a view out of the window at the trail the guys went down two hours ago.

'I haven't decided yet,' I reply because that's the truth.

'I should be the one to tell Lewis and Cole,' Kim says. 'If they have to know.'

'What do you mean if they have to know? Of course they do.'

'Do they? I don't see why ruining everybody's lives is going to make any of this better.'

'You mean you don't see why ruining your life will make it better?'

I have no time for Kim trying to protect herself in all of this. She might be making out like she is afraid for Lewis's and Cole's feelings, but I know she's just as worried for what might happen to her if the truth is told.

'Okay, fine. You hate me and you never want to see me again,' Kim says rather astutely. 'I get that. I deserve it after what I did to you. But don't ruin my family. Don't take everything I've got.'

'Cole deserves to know who his real father is,' I snap back. 'And Lewis deserves to know that he has been raising another man's son all this time.'

'What do you suppose my husband will do with that information? Shrug his shoulders and leave? Find somebody else and start another family? Or get so angry and consumed by revenge that he hurts someone?'

Kim raises her eyebrows at me as she waits for my answer, as if she thinks she has just taken the lead in this debate of ours. But she hasn't, not as I see it.

'The only person he might hurt is you, so forgive me if I don't really care about that.'

'That's not correct, and you know it. Don't you think he'd want to hurt Ryan as well?'

'Well, maybe he deserves it too.'

'Maybe he does. But does Emily deserve to have her father hurt?'

'Lewis isn't violent.'

'Isn't he? How would you know what he's like? He's my husband and I'm telling you, if he gets a shock like this, I dread to think what he might do to your husband.'

I wonder what Kim means by that. Has Lewis acted violently before? If so, to what extreme?

'Has he hurt you?' I ask nervously, and Kim lowers her head, not answering me verbally but her body language is doing the talking for her.

'Kim? What happened?'

I need to know because despite what is going on and what I plan to expose, if there is a serious danger of Lewis acting violently to anybody in a way that threatens their life then I have to factor that into my decision making.

'There was a night a couple of months ago,' Kim says quietly, her hands clasped together in her lap as she keeps her head lowered. 'He came back from work late and I could tell he'd been drinking. He'd driven home so I had a go at him for drink driving. Told him he was stupid, could have hurt someone. He told me to drop it, but I wanted to know why he had done such a reckless thing. And then he hit me.'

'What?'

Kim shakes her head. 'I was stunned. I started crying. But he went for me again and it was only when I screamed and begged him to stop that he did.'

'Was Cole in the house?'

'No, he was at a friend's place, thank God.'

'So what happened then?'

'I wanted to tell Lewis to leave but I was too scared, so I was going to go myself. But Lewis wouldn't let me. He was blocking the door and he told me that if I tried to go then he'd hit me again and I wouldn't get up this time.'

I can't believe what I'm hearing. Lewis is a lot of things, but I never had him down as a domestic abuser. Now that I know about this, it does make me rethink things a little and I guess that's why Kim told me about it.

'How come you didn't tell anybody about this at the time?' I ask her.

'I was afraid. Lewis apologised in the morning when he'd sobered up. Said it would never happen again.'

'And you believed him?'

'I don't know. I guess. He hasn't done anything since.'

'That doesn't make it right.'

'I know that.'

I feel bad for Kim but then the thought occurs to me that she could be lying about this. I mean, with all she has lied about already, what is stopping her telling one more fib?

'If he hit you in the face then how come nobody noticed the bruising?' I ask her sceptically.

'Because I covered it with make-up,' she tells me. 'It was only Cole I had to hide it from. I just avoided everybody else by cancelling plans for that week. Remember how we were supposed to go for lunch at Stefano's on that Tuesday?'

I think back a few months and recall the time when we did have a lunch date set, only for Kim to text me that morning and tell me she was feeling unwell so would have to cancel.

Maybe she is telling the truth.

This might change my approach when the guys get back, but I need to think about it, so I'm just about to head upstairs to check on Emily when I see her coming down towards me. And she has something in her hands.

'Mummy, what's this?' she asks me as she holds up the item that turns my whole body cold instantly.

'Emily, be careful with that!' I cry, rushing towards her and grabbing the gun out of her hand before holding it as far away from her as possible.

Inspecting it more closely, I see it's a handgun, the kind I've only ever seen on TV before. But now I have one in my hand and, seconds ago, my daughter was the one holding it.

'Where did you get this?' I ask Emily, my body still stone cold from seeing her with it in the first place.

'I found it in a box in the wardrobe upstairs. I was looking for something to play with.'

'Why the hell is there a gun here?'

That last question was for Kim who has rushed over to join us on the stairs, and she looks mortified.

'I don't know. I didn't know it was here!'

'Stop lying! My daughter could have died!'

'I'm sorry but I don't know why it's here! It must be Lewis's.'

'Why the hell does Lewis have a gun?'

I'm still holding the deadly weapon delicately and at arm's length like it might go off even if I don't pull the trigger.

'He's a member of a gun club.'

'What?'

'It's something one of his friends got him into. They all go shooting together every now and then at a club. But Lewis always told me the guns stayed there.'

'Well he lied because there's a gun here!'

I want to put it down, but I don't know where the best place to leave it is without my daughter picking it up again.

'Give it to me. I'll get rid of it,' Kim says, but I refuse to trust this woman or her husband now, so I tell her I'll deal with it.

'Emily, where is the box that you found it in?' I ask my daughter, figuring that the best thing to do will be to put the gun back in the box where it belongs and then keep it closed.

'I'll show you,' Emily says, and she leads me upstairs. Kim follows us but I say nothing more to her as we go because I'm simply too furious at her for having a gun in this home that my family has entered, regardless of whether she knew about it or not.

Emily leads us both to the wardrobe in her room and then points to the box on the floor.

'I found it at the back, underneath some clothes,' she says. 'Am I in trouble?'

'No, you're not, darling. I'm just glad you're okay,' I say as I kneel down and carefully place the gun back in the slot that it fits into. But I freeze when I realise there is a second slot right next to it and that one is empty.

'Is there supposed to be two guns?' I ask Kim.

'I don't know.'

'It looks like! Where is it?'

'I just said I don't know!'

The fact there might be another gun somewhere in this cabin fills me with dread and means I can't let my daughter out of my sight now, until I know for sure. But it turns out that I need not have worried because the gun wasn't in the cabin.

It's already with somebody.

Somebody out in the forest.

TWENTY-ONE

LEWIS

My backpack is lighter without the bottle of whiskey in it.

But it still feels pretty heavy with the gun in there.

I take a third swig from the bottle before handing it to the man walking beside me. Ryan looks a little unsure, as if he might already have had enough even though we've only just started, but I give him a friendly nudge until he helps himself to another mouthful. And then there's only one more member of the party who needs their turn with the bottle before it comes back to me and that would be Cole, who is walking on the other side of me.

'Are you serious?' Cole asks when he sees me holding the bottle out towards him.

'Yeah, why not? You were right the other day. I need to stop treating you like a kid.'

Cole can't take the bottle quickly enough then once he knows he's not going to get in trouble for it, but just before he can put it to his lips, Ryan expresses concern.

'Are you sure about this?' he asks me.

'Yeah, it's fine,' I say batting the air casually. 'I feel bad about what happened with the beer the other day. I overreacted.'

'This is a lot stronger than one beer,' Ryan quite rightly points out, not that I needed him to explain that to me.

'I know that, but it's fine. Come on, this is a male bonding trip. What else are three guys wandering through the forest supposed to do together but share a bottle of something strong and get things off their chest?'

I look to Cole then who takes the hint and has a drink. As I expected, the liquor overpowers him instantly and he quickly screws up his face and gags a little, but at least he managed to keep it down.

'Good lad,' I say as I swipe the bottle back from him and take another sip.

Cole is still coughing beside me, while I can feel Ryan's eyes on me as he internally questions why I would give my son such strong alcohol at his tender age. But that's the thing, isn't it?

Cole isn't my son.

He's Ryan's.

So why would I give a damn?

It could be said that I came across that awful truth very slowly but surely over the course of Cole's life, although I did have my suspicions even before he was born. That was because Kim and I had been having difficulty conceiving a child and, after a little investigation by a local fertility expert, we were told it was because I had a low sperm count. While that was disappointing to hear, I was then informed that there were things I could take to boost that count and improve my fertility and that having a child shouldn't be a problem in the long run. That all sounded well and good in the doctor's office and it sounded even better a few weeks later when Kim told me she was pregnant.

But there was one small problem.

I hadn't actually started taking the medication yet.

Of course, I thought we might have got lucky. Maybe my swimmers were better than the doctor thought. Perhaps I hadn't needed the meds after all. Surely not if Kim had already conceived and we had been trying, so it made sense and I embraced the pregnancy, looking forward to having my own child because I didn't know any better then. But, in hindsight, that was the first time I entertained the brief idea that something else might be going on.

'Another round!' I cry as I shove the bottle into Ryan's hand, causing a little whiskey to spill over the top and onto his jacket as I do.

'Wow, someone's really having a party,' Ryan says as he eyes the bottle thrust upon him. 'I'm not sure how much of this I can drink at this time of day.'

'Now who's being the boring one,' I cry, teasing him. 'Everybody's always telling me to relax and when I do they start getting uptight.'

I don't think Ryan appreciates being called boring, so he has another drink, and no sooner has he handed me the bottle than I put it into Cole's hands again.

'Hey, hang on,' Ryan says, expressing more concern. 'I don't think he should have too much more of that.'

'Why not?'

'Why do you think? He's fifteen.'

'So you think he's not man enough to handle it? You thought he could the other day when you gave him a beer, right? So what's changed?'

Ryan doesn't want to answer those tricky questions because there's no right answers there. To say yes would only encourage Cole to drink more, but to say no would make it seem like he really does view Cole as a child rather than the adult he has been trying to treat him like all weekend. But, of course, I knew this would put Ryan in an awkward position, which is why I asked such things.

Cole seems to be waiting for further permission before he has any more, but as Ryan says nothing to answer my questions, I wink at Cole to let him know that he is to go for it.

He does and once again, he ends up coughing and spluttering.

I laugh and slap him heartily on the back before telling him that I'm proud of him, but it's only a line designed to get under Ryan's skin, and it works because I see him grimace as we walk on. He's obviously feeling protective of Cole and doesn't want him to get sick and I understand that because it's exactly how I felt when Cole came into this world.

The day Cole was born was the happiest day of my life. Holding a tiny baby boy in my arms and knowing that I was one of the two people responsible for keeping him safe as he grew up was an incredibly overwhelming feeling, but it was one that gave me a strong sense of pride and purpose. It made me grow up in all areas and it certainly made me double my efforts in my fledging business as I aimed to provide the best life I could for my child.

Perhaps Cole coming on the scene was the reason my business grew so fast at the start. He certainly gave me plenty of motivation. But I guess it was also the reason I had to spend so much time away from home and, over the years, that did put a strain on both my relationship with him and with his mother. Things seemed to get worse when Cole entered his teenage years, and I found that I couldn't do anything right with him. Everything I said or did seemed to irritate him, which I was told was not an uncommon way for teenagers to be with their parents, but this felt like much more than that. It was as if we had nothing in common, nothing more to bond us together other than the fact that we were family and had to co-exist in the same house.

I couldn't shake that feeling and expressed my concerns to Kim several times, but she always assured me that Cole loved me and that I was being as good a father as he needed me to be. But, after one incident a couple of months ago in which Cole told me he hated me during another one of our arguments, I saw a look in his eye that made me wonder if he really meant it. When I said this to Kim, she got extremely uncomfortable with me raising the idea that I felt Cole and I were worlds apart. It reminded me a little of how she had been when I told her I hadn't actually started using the medication back when we found out she was pregnant and, after so many years of feeling like something was wrong in my family, I settled on the disturbing theory that Cole might not be mine.

But just thinking such a thing without ever trying to prove it would lead to nothing but sleepless nights, so I knew I had to test my theory to know for sure, one way or the other. That test came in the form of me sending away Cole's toothbrush to be used in a secretive paternity test to compare his DNA to my own. It was secretive because I didn't tell Kim what I was doing, nor did I tell Cole and I didn't need his permission either because he was under the age of sixteen. A nervous wait for the results ensued before I got the phone call I had been anxiously awaiting. And when I did, I found out the grim truth.

Cole was definitely not mine.

'Urgh, that's strong stuff,' I say, grimacing myself after a particularly large gulp of the whiskey.

'How about we save the rest of it for tonight?' Ryan suggests then, eager to get the top back on the bottle before I can give any more of it to Cole.

'Don't worry, there's plenty to go round,' I say and go to give him the bottle again.

'No, I'm fine, thank you,' he tells me.

'Whatever. Cole, you're up, buddy.'

I pass the bottle to the tipsy teenager beside me, and he tries to receive it, but Ryan swipes it out of my hand at the last second.

'Hey, what are you doing?' I cry, stumbling a little as I momentarily lose my balance, a combination of the difficult terrain underfoot and the fact I've consumed so much booze over the last twenty minutes.

'I think we should have a break,' Ryan says, keeping the bottle away from me. 'And I think Cole's definitely had enough.'

'No, I'm fine!' Cole says in between hiccups, and he looks even more unstable on his feet than I do.

'You're drunk,' Ryan says. 'And your father should know better.'

'Yeah, he should,' I snap back without skipping a beat, and my answer causes Ryan enough concern for him to hold my gaze for a moment.

'Is everything okay?' he asks me then, clearly sensing that it's not.

'Why wouldn't it be, pal?' I reply, slapping him hard on the back. 'I'm out walking in the woods with my son and my friend. What could possibly be troubling me at a time like this?'

Ryan looks uncertain before suggesting Cole walk on ahead of us a little.

Cole does as he is told for the first time in his life, and I guess whiskey was the secret ingredient to make him compliant. Only when he is a little ahead of us does Ryan speak.

'Come on, mate, I know you've got things on your mind, but I don't think this is the way to handle it,' he says, as if he thinks calling me 'mate' can make everything all right between us. But it can't and the reason for that is because I know exactly who he is now.

And he certainly isn't my mate.

After discovering the horrible truth that Cole wasn't mine, the next step was to find out whose he was. But I didn't want to just ask Kim because I feared doing that would make her go on the defensive and I might never find out. So I tried to figure it out myself by thinking about who she might have been close to around the time Cole was conceived. That gave me a few ideas, from people that she used to work with to friends of ours.

Friends like Ryan.

He was on my list, and he moved quickly to the top of it when I considered two things. One, how much time we spent around Ryan and Nicola, not only around the time the pregnancy would have been conceived but in the years that followed it. They were the people we saw the most, outside of family members. And two, just how good Ryan had always been with Cole. He was unusually attentive. Interested in his life beyond what might be considered normal. And Cole certainly seemed to respond a hell of a lot better to Ryan than he did to me.

Could it be?

Could Kim have slept with Ryan and had his son?

The more I thought about it, the more I reflected on all the trips our two families had made together over the years. At the time, I just thought it was because Kim and Nicola were best friends and wanted to see plenty of each other. But considering that it was mainly Kim who suggested such things, what if it had all been a ploy to help Ryan spend some time around Cole?

I needed to get Ryan's toothbrush.

I needed another DNA test.

After stealing the item while at Ryan and Nicola's house for a dinner date a couple of weeks ago, I sent the toothbrush off for testing and, when the results came back last week, I uncovered the depths of the deception.

I was so angry I wanted to storm around to Ryan's house and punch him as hard as I could. But I've never hit anyone in my life, and despite wanting to do it I couldn't. Also hindering my actions was the deep sense of embarrassment and pain I felt about finding out the last fifteen years had been a lie. I felt disgusted, not just with Kim and Ryan but with myself for being deceived. It was a disgust that only got worse whenever I had to look at Cole and be reminded of what an idiot I had been.

I was fairly certain that Kim and Ryan had not continued their affair after I'd spent some time both following my wife and checking her messages whenever I got the chance. That was one blessing, I suppose, though the damage had already been done years before and despite taking time to try and process it all, I could not see a way forward for myself anymore.

That was when I decided what to do.

With a weekend away already planned in Scotland with Ryan in attendance, I was going to confront him and my wife there before using one of the guns I had stolen from my gun club to disappear into the forest and take my own life. It might seem drastic, and I was certainly afraid when the thought first crossed my mind, but there was also a strange comfort to be found in it too. I was feeling so despondent and depressed thinking about my wife being a liar and my son not being mine that I knew simply confronting Kim and Ryan and filing for a divorce was not enough. I'd still have to live with the feelings of shame every day and I just knew I couldn't bear it.

I kept my depression fairly well hidden from Kim simply by working later and later and avoiding as much time around her as possible, which led to a few arguments, like her accusing me of being a workaholic but that was something she had called me many times over the years, so at least she didn't think I was acting out of the ordinary. Cole knew very little of my inner turmoil too because we'd always had a frosty relationship since he became a teenager, so a few more arguments or days with only a few words spoken between us didn't make much of a difference.

The more I considered my decisive course of action the more I felt it was the perfect way to conclude this sorry matter. Everybody would know why I had done it and the truth would be exposed about Kim and Ryan, but at least I would be spared having to be around to deal with the fallout from it. I would just take myself away at some point over the weekend and deal with my problem in my own way, out of sight of everybody, especially the kids. I knew it would take some great acting on my part to keep it hidden until the moment I was ready to expose the lies, but for maximum impact, I knew it was best to let Kim and Ryan think they were getting away with it right in front of me, until suddenly I told them that they weren't. Imagine the guilt they would feel once I had taken my own life. That would be far stronger than simply having a few arguments with them and then leaving them alone. They would have to live with the guilt forever and, maybe, if I got lucky, it would eat them alive like their lies have ultimately eaten me alive. I hope it ruins their lives just like my life is ruined too, now that I can't bear going on while knowing the horrible truth.

Even so, such a drastic course of action is not simple to carry out and it took me a while to pluck up the courage over the course of the weekend. We were on day two before I was starting to feel anywhere near like I was ready to act. I mostly spent that time drinking as much as I could to try and give myself a false sense of courage that I could carry out my plan. But then Cole went and flattened the battery on the car and the distraction it provided gave me a little more time to think about things. When I did, I realised that it wasn't right if I was the only one to leave this world this weekend. No, I should take somebody else with me, somebody who deserved to die a lot more than I did.

Somebody like the lying, cheating man standing right next to me now.

TWENTY-TWO

NICOLA

The box with one gun in it is now safely secured and stored away from where Emily or anybody else might stumble across it. But there is still one gun missing and that's what's troubling me now as I continue to ask Kim where it might be.

'I don't know,' she tells me as she stands sheepishly in front of the kitchen counter while I pace around between her and Emily, who is sitting on the sofa with the TV on quietly in the background.

'Lewis must have it,' I suggest.

'Maybe. Or maybe he only stole one gun from his club.'

'But the box has two spaces for two guns, and one is missing!'

'I know that, but it doesn't mean both guns came here!'

Kim could be right, but the uncertainty is killing me.

'I still don't understand why he would even bother to bring one gun here!' I cry. 'Does he not know how dangerous that is?'

'Like I said, I had no idea he had a gun!'

'But he does and there's potentially another one out there somewhere! So where is it and what is he planning to do with it?'

It's almost beyond belief that Lewis would bring a weapon on holiday with another family but for him to do that suggests there was some reasoning behind it. I'm still thinking about what Kim told me regarding her husband and how he had been violent with her recently, and now I know he is the kind of person who likes to be around guns, my paranoia about how he might react to the shocking news I have for him is heightened even further.

How can I tell him who Cole's real dad is now?

And that's when I think of something truly terrifying.

'What if he already knows?'

My question to Kim is met with silence as she struggles to catch up to my thinking.

'What?'

'Lewis! What if he already knows about Cole?'

'What about Cole?' Emily asks, clearly not as distracted by the television as I thought she was. If I could, I would have had her in another room so Kim and I could have this conversation privately, but I'm not letting Emily out of my sight now I know this is the kind of place that has dangerous weapons lurking within its rooms. So she has to be here, although I still don't want her to know about Ryan, Cole and this whole sorry mess yet.

'Nothing. It doesn't matter,' I tell my daughter. 'Just watch the TV.'

I grab the remote control and turn the volume up a little more so she can't hear us as well.

'He doesn't know,' Kim tells me quietly, referring to Lewis.

'Are you sure about that?'

'Yes, I'm positive.'

'You didn't think I knew until an hour ago though, did you?'

My good point shuts Kim up for a second.

'So what if there is some way that Lewis found out the truth. Is it possible?'

'No, I don't think so.'

'Let's just say it is for a moment. What do you think he would do if he did know Cole wasn't his?'

I almost whispered that so there's no chance Emily heard me and when I glance at her, she is still watching the loud television.

'It's a stupid question because he doesn't know,' Kim replies adamantly.

'But if he does know then he might have taken a gun with him today and he might be planning to use it to get revenge on Ryan, right?'

I try to stay calm as I speak but it's a frightening thought. I'm as angry at Ryan as anybody but I wouldn't want him to get shot. Nor would I want anybody else to get seriously hurt. But now I have put the thought in Kim's mind, there is only one person she is worried about.

'Cole!' she says, suddenly realising what I figured out two minutes ago: that Lewis might know the truth and might be planning something horrible today. 'I need to go and find them now!'

'Wait!'

I grab her before she can rush away from me and force her to think this through.

'We don't know for sure that Lewis is going to use the gun. He might not even have it with him. But if he does, we can't just go running out into the forest calling his name.'

'I just want to make sure Cole is okay,' Kim says, the fear on her face familiar because it's the same fear I've had whenever I've worried Emily has been in danger in the past, although never to this extreme.

'I understand. But Lewis wouldn't hurt Cole.'

'He would if he wants to get back at me.'

Kim has a point, and I can't argue otherwise. All I can do is urge her to try and stay calm. But it's no good. Now I have put the thought in her head that Lewis might know what I discovered yesterday, all she can think about is trying to find Cole to make sure he is all right.

'I'm going,' she tells me before she runs upstairs and disappears for a moment. When she comes back, she has her running trainers on and her coat in her hand.

'Are you coming with me?' she asks me as she pulls on her coat quickly.

I think about it but then I look at Emily and realise that, just like Kim, my priority has to be to keep my child safe.

'No,' I tell her. 'We're staying here.'

'Fine,' Kim says, and she rushes to the door to leave.

I almost call after her and tell her to be careful, but our relationship is not the same any more and I can't pretend I care about her as much as I once did.

'Where's she going, Mummy?' Emily asks me as Kim exits and the cabin door slams behind her.

'She's just going to find the others,' I say, tentatively walking over to the glass door and looking out of it.

As I do, I see Kim running down the trail before disappearing into the trees, and once she's gone, I wonder how long it will take her to find the guys.

I also wonder what might be waiting for her when she does.

TWENTY-THREE

RYAN

I might have failed in persuading Lewis to take it a little easier with the whiskey bottle but at least I have been able to stop him giving any more to Cole. The teenager has already drunk far too much and while he might be finding his tipsy state quite pleasant, I'm not and I doubt he will be for much longer if any nausea kicks in. But, for now, Cole is relatively okay. He is walking just behind me, while Lewis is ahead, the open bottle still in his hand.

I decided it wasn't wise to get into too much of an argument with him out here in the middle of this forest over his clear substance abuse, because for one I need him to help direct us back to the cabin. I have absolutely no idea which way we need to go, so he's my only guide out here. Better to not aggravate him too much then.

I'm still reeling from his confession that his business is failing, almost as much as I am about him telling me that he is envious of how I am with Cole. With all that going on in his head, it's little wonder Lewis feels the need to drown out some of his thoughts with hard liquor, but it would be nice if he could keep himself in a relatively sober state long enough to get us back to the cabin.

Looking around, I fail to recognise this part of the forest as one we passed through when we were heading in the other direction on the way to the main road. Then again, it all looks the same around here. Just trees, trees and more trees. This must be the right way because Lewis knows his way around here.

Or at least he did before he opened that bottle.

He starts singing then, a song I don't recognise, not that I would join in with him even if I did. His voice is loud alongside the only other sound out here, which is our feet trampling over all the dense foliage. I definitely don't remember it being this difficult to traverse earlier.

Is this really the same way we came before?

I'm just about to ask Lewis when I see him trip and fall right in front of me, the bottle flying from his hands and disappearing in the bushes, which might be for the best.

'Are you okay?' I ask the fallen man, rushing over to where he lies and praying that he hasn't sprained an ankle or done anything else that might make it impossible for him to walk back to the cabin. But when I get there, Lewis just rolls onto his back and can't stop laughing, as if he has the giggles, which is a rather strange way of being after falling over. He's slightly hysterical, maniacal even and it's very unnerving.

'Dad, are you okay?' Cole asks, clearly just as worried as I am about Lewis, but his use of the D-word stings when I hear it.

'Don't worry about me,' Lewis says, still chuckling. 'Just find that bottle.'

Cole sets off to look for it, but I stop him.

'It's gone, mate. We won't find it in all these bushes and even if we do, it'll probably be empty now if the top was off. Never mind, let's just get you back and you can have a drink then.'

I go to help Lewis up, but he pushes me off him and I almost fall over myself thanks to the shove he just gave me.

'Hey! I'm trying to help you!' I cry.

'I don't need your help,' Lewis replies gruffly and then it's Cole's turn to offer a hand.

But what Lewis says next surprises me even more.

'And I don't need your help either, thank you very much.'

His rejection of Cole is not just strange, it's downright rude, as if there is real passion behind him telling the youngster that he doesn't need him.

Cole looks hurt, as one might expect a son to be when their father has just been so awful to them, and seeing my boy being treated like that ignites a flame in me that I will do well to control. I want to admonish Lewis for his behaviour, and despite knowing it might be better to just leave it, I can't help it.

'Hey, don't talk to him like that,' I say. 'It's not his fault you've had too much to drink and lost your balance.'

'Isn't it?' Lewis says as he gets back to his feet, his backpack loosely hanging off one of his shoulders.

'No, of course not.'

'I beg to differ. I think it is his fault. But I think it's mainly yours.'

I have no idea what Lewis means but I don't like the way he is looking at me. That's why I suggest we just keep moving. But Lewis doesn't want to go anywhere.

'Didn't you hear me? I said this is *your* fault,' Lewis says, jabbing a finger in my direction. 'All of it.'

'What are you talking about?'

I'm tired of his moods now, but also afraid of where this anger is really coming from.

'I'm talking about what you have done behind my back. You and my wife!'

I swear my heart skips a beat at that moment, as if my body

has reacted instantly to hearing that Lewis might know what happened between Kim and I all those years ago.

But he can't know about it, right?

'Lewis, I have no idea what you are talking about. I just want to get back to the cabin, so how about we keep moving.'

I set off then in what I presume is the right direction we need to be going in, but I've barely made it five yards before Lewis says the worst thing he could have possibly said in the situation.

'I know Cole is not my son.'

I freeze, too afraid to turn back to look at both Lewis and Cole behind me, but also aware that I can't just carry on walking away now that the truth has been exposed. This is it. The moment I'd been trying to avoid all of Cole's life. The moment when my and several other people's lives will now change forever.

'Wait, what?' Cole says, no doubt as confused as anybody would be in his situation.

'I'm sorry, but you have to know,' Lewis says. 'You deserve to know, just like everybody else does.'

'Lewis, stop,' I say, finding my voice then and turning back to face him, as well as the shocked Cole, my hands out in front of myself as if defending my body, but it's not from a dangerous weapon. It's from words. I am trying to fend off any more truths that could come from Lewis's mouth.

'It's too late for that,' he says with a shake of the head, but I urge him to reconsider.

'No, it's not. You don't have to do this. Not here. Not anywhere.'

I'm well past the point of giving a damn about how Lewis might have found out Cole isn't his and more focused on just getting Lewis to shut up before he can ruin my life and confuse poor Cole even more. But there's little I can do to stop a man who is clearly intent on delivering brutal honesty today.

'Dad, what is going on?' Cole asks Lewis, still referring to him by that name even though he's just heard Lewis say Cole is not his.

'Don't call me that, son,' Lewis replies then, tears filling his eyes and his voice shaking slightly. 'You can't call me that any more because I'm not your dad. I wish I was, but I'm not.'

'I don't understand.'

Now Cole is getting upset and this is all getting very dangerously out of hand. What I can't understand is, even if Lewis has found out the truth, why he would choose to reveal it here of all places. There has to be a more considerate time and place than this and it's mainly Cole I'm thinking about now.

'Lewis, please. Don't do this,' I say, urging a man who has no right to show me some compassion to suddenly do just that. But as I feared, it doesn't work.

'I'm not your father,' Lewis says to Cole, looking and sounding distraught as he speaks. 'But that man is.'

He points to me then and that's the moment Cole discovers who I really am.

'This doesn't make any sense,' he says, staring at me with wide, disbelieving eyes. 'What is going on?'

'I've just told you. Ryan is your dad, not me. Isn't that right, Ryan?'

'Lewis, please.'

'Admit it!'

Lewis's loud cry echoes across the wide-open space we're standing in the middle of and even manages to send a few birds fluttering from the tops of the trees.

I can't bring myself to do what I've just been told, but as Cole keeps looking at me, his eyes watering and his diminutive frame shaking, I feel I have no choice.

So I nod my head.

'It's true,' I say solemnly.

Cole begins to tremble even more then, but he needs proof and asks for it.

'I have the DNA results in a box at home,' Lewis says sadly. 'That's all the proof you'll need.'

I'm expecting Cole to start asking me questions or call me names or say something to let me know that he hates me and the lies that have been told to him all his life. But he doesn't do any of that.

Instead, he just turns and runs.

'Cole! Come back!' I cry before going after him, but I know it'll be hard work trying to keep up with him as he races ahead of me because he is much faster than I am.

But it gets even harder when Lewis tells me to stay where I am or he'll shoot.

I look back and, when I do, I see Lewis pointing a gun right at me, his arm straight and his finger on the trigger, looking every bit like he means what he just said.

'What the hell! Where did you get a gun from?' I cry before glancing back to where Cole was to make sure he is not in the firing line. But he's already disappeared, lost amongst the trees as he runs away, not towards the cabin but as far away as possible from the two men who have just given him an awful truth.

'We need to go after Cole!' I try, hoping Lewis will come to his senses and realise this is about the boy's wellbeing now.

'You're not going anywhere,' he tells me calmly, the gun still aimed squarely at my chest. 'Take one step and I'll kill you.'

'Lewis, please. Don't do this. You're not a killer.'

'I'm a man who has got nothing to lose.'

Is there anything scarier than that?

'Look, I'm sorry for what I did,' I say, speaking fast now because I'm not sure how long I have. 'And I'm sorry about your business problems. I'm sorry about everything that has happened, but this isn't the right way to deal with it. Don't throw everything away over me. I don't deserve it.'

I mean that, which hurts me but does little to calm down the man with the gun.

'I don't want to go on living with all of this,' Lewis says. 'But there's no way you should be allowed to go on living either.'

That's the moment I realise there is nothing I can say to stop him doing what he is planning to do, so I put my hands out in front of myself and close my eyes, preparing for the end to come.

I just hope it will be quick and painless.

And then I hear Kim's voice, calling out for both me and Cole through the trees, and the unexpected noise is just enough to distract Lewis long enough for him to lower his gun slightly.

When he does, I turn and run for my life.

TWENTY-FOUR

NICOLA

I've lost track of how long it's been since Kim ran out of this cabin, because I've been keeping myself busy ever since by packing everything up so we can make a quick exit out of here as soon as the car is fixed.

I'm throwing all my clothes into my suitcase as quickly as possible, as well as scooping up all my toiletry items from the ensuite and showing far less care for their storage as I did when I packed them in the first place. I couldn't care less if everything gets crumpled, creased or possibly even damaged on the way home. I'm not even that bothered if I accidentally leave something behind. I just need to get as much of this stuff together as I can so I don't waste any time later. But it's not easy with a little girl following me around and asking so many questions.

Emily won't stop trying to get me to tell her what is going on, even though I've already tried getting her to leave it several times. She might be young but she's not stupid and she knows Kim and I have been arguing, as well as this all having something to do with the guys that Kim has now gone to find. I'm aware that trying to protect her from the truth for as long as possible is only delaying the inevitable and I'll have to tell her everything one day, but not today.

'Emily, for goodness' sake. How many times do I have to tell you? Stop asking me questions and go and finish packing your things!'

I seem to finally get through to her, unfortunately having to shout very loudly in the process, as Emily skulks out of the room and does as I say.

With her out of the way, it's a little easier to make progress and once my suitcase is full, I haul it out of the bedroom and take it downstairs, depositing it by the front door ready to be packed into the trunk of the car very shortly. Then I think about tidying up a little around the place, noting some of the dirty plates on the side as well as evidence of crisps wrappers, drinks cartons and other miscellaneous items littering some of the surfaces in here. But then I remember that there's no need for me to be polite now. Who gives a damn about leaving a little mess behind considering what's happened since I've been here?

'Emily, how are you getting on up there?'

My call upstairs goes unanswered, so I have to go and investigate and when I do, I find Emily lying on her bed reading her book.

'What are you doing? I told you to finish packing! We have to go soon!'

'No, I'm not doing it,' Emily says, proving to be as stubborn as I can be and that's my girl, although I don't feel much pride about that fact at the moment.

'What do you mean you're not doing it? You don't have a choice! I'm telling you!'

'No, I'm not going until you tell me why everyone is in a bad mood.'

'Nobody's in a bad mood!'

'Is it something I've done?'

'What? No, of course not!'

'I don't want to go. I like it here. It's nicer than at home.'

'But it's not our place so we have to go. Emily, please, just do as I say.'

Emily very slowly and very deliberately closes her book before getting off the bed, but she isn't huffing or puffing like I might expect her to be after she hasn't gotten her own way. Instead, she is very quiet and that is more troubling because I know it means something is wrong.

'What is it?' I ask her as I watch her gather up some of her things.

'I'm scared.'

'What are you scared about?'

'The gun.'

'You don't have to worry about that. The gun is gone now. You're safe. So am I.'

'And Daddy?'

How can I answer that?

'Yes, Daddy is safe too.'

'But what if he gets shot?'

'He won't get shot.'

'But he might.'

'No, he won't. Now come on, let's keep packing.'

I give Emily some help then in getting the rest of her belongings into her small suitcase, but I can't shake the troubling concern from my mind that she has just raised.

What if Ryan does get shot? If Lewis does have the other gun with him then there's a good reason he took it with them on their walk, and I doubt it has anything to do with needing it in case they encountered any trouble on route. It's not as if this is a dangerous part of the world.

Maybe he took it to shoot a deer. A little hunting? Could that be it? That might be the best-case scenario and it's what I'll tell myself the gun could only be used for as we finish packing and I lift Emily's suitcase from her bed.

'Is this everything?'

'Yeah.'

'Okay, let's go downstairs.'

I lead Emily to the doorway, but she tells me she needs the bathroom and I can't really argue with her considering what has been happening with her body recently.

'Okay, that's fine. I'll take your bag down and I'll see you when you're ready. Call me if you need me and don't lock the door.'

Emily heads into the bathroom while I go downstairs and put her bag beside mine. I'm aware there is one bag missing, Ryan's, but he can pack his own damn things. The day I stopped doing things for that man was the day I found out he was a cheating liar.

With Emily upstairs and everyone else out, the cabin is deathly quiet and as I stand and wallow in the silence, I think about all the people I'm going to see when I get home. As I do, I wonder how I'm ever going to tell them what's going on. My parents. My friends. Work colleagues. I can't act as if everything is all right around them, not when I'm planning on leaving Ryan and certainly not when I actually do. They'll want answers and if I give them, they'll recoil in shock.

Nobody wants to be the one who everyone pities, but how else are they all supposed to feel towards me when they find out my husband cheated on me and fathered another child, a fact he managed to keep quiet from me for over fifteen years? I'll get so much sympathy as well as plenty of hugs and concerned expressions, and I'm sure it will be all very well meaning. But there's a problem and it's that I don't want any of it.

I don't want my mum to have to keep checking on me every day to ask if I'm all right or my dad to come and help deal with some of the logistics involved in me setting up life as a single parent. I don't want to be drowning in a sea of cups of teas from all the people who offer to make me one, each of them just as worried as the last about my mental state and how I'm managing to survive, while gossiping about me once they've left and saying that I don't deserve such bad luck. There may even be the need for me to have some time off work and I'm sure my employer would be very understanding, but I'd rather just go and carry on my job like I used to, although that seems fanciful now with so much on my mind.

I don't want any of that but I'm going to get it all if I leave Ryan, explain why I've done that and try and figure out how to move forward while managing my broken heart. For that reason, even though I want to get as far away from this cabin as possible, for the time being I'm also kind of enjoying the fact that I'm still here, surrounded by silence and not having to face anybody's sympathies just yet.

I hear the call of a bird outside and it makes me jump a little having grown so used to the stillness here. That's followed quickly by the sound of a branch snapping somewhere nearby in the forest, and I wonder if it could be somebody returning to the cabin. And then I hear a third sound, one I wish I had never heard and one that makes me almost jump out of my skin.

It's a gunshot. Unmistakable. A trigger was just pulled, and a bullet was just fired.

Oh my God, it must have been Lewis. He must have used the weapon he took with him. But who has he shot at? Ryan? Cole? Kim? Or himself?

'Mum! What was that?' Emily calls out to me, and I go racing up the stairs to make sure she is okay, even though I feel the gunshot was some distance away from us here. But it was still close enough to startle the pair of us, and when I enter the bathroom, I find Emily looking very disturbed.

'It's okay, darling,' I tell her, taking her hand. 'Come on, let's go.'

I lead her out of the bathroom but I'm almost afraid to go downstairs in case Lewis comes back with the gun still in his hand. That's why I decide to take Emily to the ensuite bathroom in my bedroom and figure we can wait there, locking the door if we need to depending on who comes back and what mood they are in when they get here.

But just before we reach the ensuite, I think about the gun I safely stored away a short time ago. Maybe it wouldn't be a bad idea if I was to take it again and keep it on me, just in case we have to defend ourselves soon.

Having to try and keep my daughter safe by arming myself is a horrible prospect, but better to be safe than sorry, so I return to where I hid the gun, and after telling Emily to stay back, I open the box to take the weapon out.

But when I do, I find the box empty.

'Emily! Have you been in this box?' I cry, terrified of her risking harming herself again, but she is adamant that she hasn't.

So if I haven't been in here and Emily hasn't either then that only leaves one person who could have taken the gun.

Kim.

She must have armed herself before she left the cabin.

But why?

TWENTY-FIVE

COLE

Two minutes before the gunshot

I pick myself up off the ground and force myself on again, desperate to get as far away from the two men behind me as possible. But it's hard to run fast in this forest and I keep falling over, tripping on branches and tree stumps and hitting the ground hard when I do. It's also tough to see where I'm going with tears in my eyes, but I can't stop crying as I go either.

What is going on? Why is this happening?

Who the hell is my dad?

In my confusion, I've managed to get lost and as I pause and look around me, I have no idea where I am now. I can't find my way to the cabin, but I don't want to stop either and let Lewis or Ryan catch up to me. So I just pick a direction and start running again.

I thought I was quite fit with all the football I play at school, but this is a lot harder than just running on grass and I stumble again, this time hitting my knee on a jagged stump, and it causes me to cry out in pain.

I grip my knee tightly and see a tear in my jeans. I bet it's bleeding under there too, but this is no time to be soft and cry out for help. I'm too angry for that and I don't want help from anybody. Maybe there isn't anyone who can help me anyway.

Has my whole life been a lie? If it has then I guess nobody really cares about me. They're all as bad as each other. Mum as well. Why am I the last to find out?

I get back to my feet and force myself onwards, but my knee really hurts, and I can't run any more. Hobbling is the best I can do, just like the time I had to come off the pitch in the big school match because I had an injury there too. I hated that day, but I hate this one more and as I keep moving, I try to figure out how any of this could be true.

How could Ryan be my real dad? I barely know him. He's just some friend of the family who I see every couple of weeks whenever the adults get together. Yeah, he's pretty cool, I suppose, but he's not my dad. *Is he?*

I thought Dad was Lewis, the guy who is always telling me not to do things and always shouting at me. That's who a dad is, isn't it? If Lewis isn't my father then why has he been there all my life? What was the point?

What's the point of any of it?

I pause and rest against a tree for a minute to get my breath back and give my knee a break. Looking back over my shoulder, I'm afraid I'll see someone coming, but I don't. Maybe I've lost them. I should be faster than them, even after my injury.

Good, I hope I never have to see either of them again.

I hate them. Both of them. They're both liars. Why would I ever forgive them for all of this, whatever the truth is? I don't need either of them. I'll be fine on my own. I'll be sixteen soon and can do what I want and what I want is to never see any of them again.

Even though I wish that was true, I know I need them to help me get out of here. Even if I get back to the cabin, I'm still stuck because I can't just take the car and drive home. I don't know how to drive and even if I did, I don't know the right way to go. And of course the car is broken, so it's pointless anyway.

Stupid Scotland. I hate it here.

The fact that I'm still dependent on the people who have lied to me makes me so frustrated that I hit out at the tree I'm leaning on, and I keep hitting it until small pieces of bark fly off.

Great, now I've got bloody knuckles to go with my bloody knee. But I've not got time to worry about that when I hear a voice behind me in the forest.

But it's not Lewis or Ryan. It's Mum. What's she doing out here? Has she come to tell me more lies? I don't want to see her either, so I push off from the tree and carry on, heading down a small slope and feeling my knee ache as it takes the full weight of my body again.

Mum calls out again. She says my name, then Lewis's and then Ryan's. But nobody answers her, so I guess she isn't able to find us yet.

If they're all out here in the forest with me then maybe I can get back to the cabin first and at least lock myself in the bathroom there. I could stay in there for as long as I want to then, ignoring them all and just being by myself. I think I'll do that. It's better than running around out here forever.

I feel better when I see a small clearing in the forest that I recognise. I've been through here before so I must be back on the right track. I'm still quite far from the cabin but at least I know where I'm going again now.

And then I realise that I'm no longer alone.

I hear the person coming first, twigs snapping under their feet as they get closer. They're approaching from my left and they're almost here.

I need to hide.

Fast.

Crouching down between two trees, I grit my teeth as I hope I've done a good job of staying out of view of whoever is going to come into this clearing in a moment's time. But every second I'm in this position causes my knee to throb and I'm not sure how long I can maintain it for.

'Cole! Cole!'

It's Ryan and I can see him now, emerging from the trees and looking around for me. He looks desperate to find me, as if he has to talk to me and explain everything. But it's too late for that, so I stay hidden.

'Cole! Where are you?' Ryan tries again. 'I'm sorry! You weren't supposed to find out like this! I'm so sorry!'

Ryan carries on and, for a second, I think I'm going to successfully avoid him. That's until my knee buckles and I cry out in pain, giving my position away and causing Ryan to come running towards me.

'Cole! Are you okay?' he asks me as I stand up straight again, gripping my knee and wishing it didn't hurt so much.

I don't want to say anything, but it doesn't matter because he's found me now, and as he reaches me, he asks me if I'm okay again.

'Just leave me alone!' I tell him. 'Get away from me!'

Ryan can tell that I mean it and keeps his distance, but he doesn't walk away like I want him to. He just keeps apologising again before telling me he can explain.

'I'm sorry. You don't deserve any of this. But if you'll just listen to me then I'll tell you why I did what I did. Why I kept it a secret all this time.'

'I don't care! I don't want to hear it!' I say, even though that's not quite true. I should hear the full story because maybe I'll understand better then. But all I want to do is make Ryan, Lewis and anybody feel the pain I am currently feeling and the only way I can think to do that is to push them away.

'Okay, that's fine. I understand,' Ryan says, rather surprisingly. 'But it's not safe here. We need to go.'

'What are you talking about?'

Now it's Ryan who is looking over his shoulder as if he doesn't want to get caught by anybody either.

'It's Lewis,' he says in between heavy breaths. 'He's got a gun.'

'What?'

'We need to go right now. Stick with me. I'll keep you safe.'

Ryan grabs my arm and tries to pull me away, but I push him off.

'I'm not going anywhere with you!'

'We don't have time for this! Did you not hear me? Lewis has a gun and he almost shot me a moment ago!'

'Stop lying to me!'

'I'm not!'

We both freeze when we hear someone else approaching the clearing, and the fear on Ryan's face says he might be telling the truth after all. But it's too late now because Lewis is here and when I see him, I see the gun in his hand too.

'Get away from him!' Lewis cries when he sees Ryan beside me. 'Leave Cole alone!'

The gun is now aimed at Ryan, who puts his hands up quickly to defend himself.

'Lewis! Drop the gun! Cole might get hurt!'

'I won't hurt him!' Lewis cries. 'You're the one I want!'

Ryan suddenly steps in front of me as if to shield me from any bullets, but there won't be any. Will there?

'Stop it!' I cry, hoping that might be enough to get Lewis to lower the weapon. But it doesn't work, and the gun is still pointed at the man standing in front of me.

'Get away from Ryan!' Lewis tells me then.

'No! Stay where you are!' Ryan quickly orders me, and I don't know what to do so I just stay still, afraid to make a movement either way.

'I swear to God, I'll shoot you,' Lewis says to Ryan as the gun shakes, but I wonder how he could ever aim properly because he looks drunk and he's so angry. I can't believe Ryan is even willing to try him.

'Stop it! Please!' I beg because I feel like I might be the only one who can stop this now. But even that doesn't work and as Lewis's finger goes tighter on the trigger, I'm terrified Ryan is about to die.

And then I see the gun get lowered inexplicably at the last moment.

It looks like Lewis isn't going to shoot after all.

Maybe everything is going to be okay, and nobody is going to die.

And then I hear a gunshot.

TWENTY-SIX

RYAN

I close my eyes before Lewis has the chance to fire, and when I hear the gunshot I expect death to come quickly. But when I realise that I'm still okay, I figure he must have missed me. That is until I open my eyes and see that he hasn't fired his gun at all. Instead, he's face down on the ground and not moving and, if anything, it looks like he's the one who has been shot.

And he has.

I immediately know this because there is another gun on the scene, and it is pointing right where Lewis once stood.

He has been hit by a bullet.

And it's his wife who has pulled the trigger.

Kim's eyes are wide as she stares at the body on the ground, her arm still raised and her right hand still holding the gun.

She just saved my life and, in doing so, she took that of her husband's.

'Mum?' Cole says behind me, and that's the thing that snaps Kim out of her trance and brings her back into the moment. When she sees her son then she drops her gun immediately and rushes towards him, but Cole only lets her get so close before he tells her to get away from him just like he told me earlier.

'What have you done?' Cole cries. 'You've killed him!'

'He was going to shoot!' Kim says. 'I had to do it.'

'Your mum's right,' I say, defending her actions. 'He was going to kill us.'

'No, he wasn't!' Cole cries, seemingly believing it. 'He lowered his gun!'

'What?'

I don't know what he means because the last thing I saw was Lewis pointing his weapon right at me.

'We're safe now,' Kim says, seemingly ignoring what Cole just said, but maybe that's the right play. We need to give the teenager a second to calm down, and while we do that I can try to figure out how we sort out this mess. A dead body is not something that is easily explained, but when the police come, we'd better be able to do just that.

'Is he definitely dead?' I ask, looking at the body a dozen yards away from where we stand.

'I think so,' Kim mumbles.

'You murdered him!' Cole cries. 'You killed Dad!'

He's jabbing his finger at Kim as he speaks, and I'm almost as shocked at him directing his anger at her as I am at him still referring to Lewis as his dad. I guess it's going to take a long time before he calls me that instead.

But, before that, I realise that we have to check the body before we go any further, so I cautiously approach Lewis, aware that while the gun has fallen from his hand, it is still close to where he lies, so if he is alive then it won't take much for him to reach out and have another go at shooting me. That's why I kick it away from him, although once I get closer to the body, I realise it doesn't matter anyway.

Lewis is definitely dead. There's blood all around him and while I can't see the wound at first, I soon find it in his chest. That must have been where Kim's bullet hit him.

His eyes are wide open and lifeless, and after I make a check for a pulse in his neck, I find that there is none. Once that's confirmed, I sink to my knees and can finally relax. But only for a second because while one nightmare is now over, another one is just beginning. I might have just dodged death but this is still far from being over. A man is dead and now we have to process that shock before we can figure out what to do about it.

Kim is having another go at talking to Cole, but he is still shouting at her to stay away from him. While they are busy fighting with each other, I'm busy trying to figure out how the police won't arrest Kim when they get here. She shot Lewis and now he's dead, so what does that mean for her? And if she's behind bars, what does it mean for Cole, who will have not only lost the man he thought was his father but his mother too?

'Stop arguing and listen to me for a minute!' I cry, getting back to my feet and marching over to the arguing pair. 'We don't have time for this. We have to call the police so they can come out here. The longer we leave it, the more suspicious it will look.'

I think that sounds like a good plan, but Kim has something she wants to add.

'But it's not suspicious. It was self-defence. I shot him before he could shoot you.'

Kim might have a point, but will the police believe that, particularly with what has just come out about who Cole's real father is? And it's even worse when Cole protests, saying that it wasn't self-defence at all and maintaining his belief that Lewis lowered his weapon before he got shot.

If only I hadn't closed my eyes then I might have been able to see for myself, but I genuinely thought Lewis was about to kill me so I was bracing myself for what was to come, meaning I missed what actually happened. But now I need answers.

'I need to talk to you for a minute,' I say to Kim. 'Cole, wait there.'

I lead Kim away from Cole so that he won't be able to hear what we're about to discuss and then I express my concerns.

'Did Lewis lower his gun before you shot him?' I ask her, afraid of what the answer might be.

'I don't know.'

'What do you mean you don't know?'

'It all happened too quickly!'

'Either he did, or he didn't. You shot him so you must have seen what he was doing!'

'I panicked! I thought he was going to shoot Cole!'

While that might be a valid reason for her pulling the trigger so decisively, it still worries me that Lewis had lowered his weapon in the seconds before she fired. If so, it sounds less like self-defence and more like murder.

'What the hell are we going to tell the police?' I ask her, holding my hands on my head and staring at the body.

'We tell them it was self-defence.'

'But it wasn't! You know it and Cole definitely knows it!'

'I was just trying to help you both. I thought he was going to kill you!'

'So did I!'

This is crazy but what is also crazy is that Kim was out here not long after I discovered that Lewis knew the truth about us. Why was she here?

'Lewis knew about me being Cole's father,' I tell her. 'That's why he was trying to kill me,' I say, but Kim isn't half as shocked as I expect her to be.

'I had a feeling he might have known. That's why I came,' she replies quietly.

'What? How could you have known?'

'Because Nicola just told me she knew too.'

The ground suddenly feels very unsteady beneath my feet. 'What? How?'

The thought of my wife knowing my darkest secret is unbearable.

'She overheard us talking in the hot tub yesterday and she confronted me on our picnic. She didn't say that Lewis knew too, but he must have found out somehow.'

'Oh my God, I need to get back to her now.'

Suddenly, my concern is my wife rather than the dead body. The mother of my daughter must hate me now and if there's any way I can change that, then I need to start working on it right now. But Kim grabs my arm before I can go.

'We need to sort this out! We need to get our story straight for the police!'

'I need to make sure my wife is okay before I do anything,' I try, but Kim still won't let me go, desperate and afraid but that's what happens when you kill somebody, I guess.

'Nicola is at the cabin with Emily and they're both fine. But we won't be unless we sort this out. I don't want to go to prison for this and I won't as long as we all say the same thing. He was going to shoot at you and Cole, so I shot him first. Right?'

That is nowhere near the full story and Kim knows it. But what choice do we have? It's either that or risk Kim going away for a very long time, and where would that leave Cole then?

'Hang on a minute. The police are going to want to know why Lewis was going to shoot us in the first place. What do we say to that?'

'I guess we have to tell them the truth.'

'That he had just found out I was the father of the boy he thought was his son? Okay, well that sure gives him motive to kill me. But what were you doing out here with a gun? How did you know he had a gun?'

'Emily found a gun in the cabin.'

'*What?*'

The thought of my precious daughter being around a gun might just be the scariest thing that has happened to me today and that includes staring down the barrel of one myself.

'How the hell did Emily find a gun?'

'Lewis must have brought them to the cabin. She found one, but we saw there was one missing. Then we guessed Lewis must have it with him in the forest.'

'So you took the other gun and ran out here to find us?'

'Yes.'

As we discuss this, I'm also thinking about how the police are going to take it. It's quite the version of events and considering they are trained to be sceptical and explore every possibility rather than just accepting the first story they get told, I'm worried they might have lots of questions. Questions like: was it just luck that Kim found us and shot Lewis in time, or was it actually planned for him to die all along and we are just making it seem like he was going to hurt us first?

'There's a problem here,' I say grimly. 'And it's what Cole and Nicola might say to the police.'

'What do you mean?'

'Well, if they tell them the truth about us having had an affair and me being Cole's real father, what if the police think that might have given us the motive to kill Lewis so we could be together?'

'What? That's ridiculous!'

'I know that, but will they?'

'Yes, they have to, because it's not true. It was just lucky that I killed him before he killed you!'

'But the police will already know we're liars thanks to Nicola and Cole. So what if they think we're lying to them again.'

'They won't!'

'But what if Cole tells them it wasn't self-defence!'

'He wouldn't do that. I'm his mum! Wouldn't you, Cole?'

We both turn to look at the teenager then, hopeful that he will confirm what really happened here and give the police less chance of not believing us. But when we look at the area he was just standing in, we realise he isn't there any more.

'Cole!' Kim cries, rushing towards the spot where he once stood.

'Come on, we need to find him,' I say. 'He can't have gone far.'

'What about Lewis?'

That's a good point. Can we really just leave a body out here in the middle of nowhere? Then again, it's hardly as if anyone is likely to stumble across it while we're gone. We haven't seen a single soul since we got up here.

'I'll come back here soon. We need to find Cole and make sure he doesn't say anything stupid to anyone.'

We set off in pursuit of our son then, both of us scarcely believing the consequences of what we set in motion all those years ago with our stupid, ill-fated one-night stand. If someone had said what we did would have not only resulted in having to keep a terrible secret for fifteen years but also having to deal with a dead body then I'd have sent for the men in white coats to take them away. But it turns out that we're the crazy ones.

I'm full of fear that Cole might make it back to the cabin before us and say something to Nicola about what happened, something that might make this situation worse for us, so it's a huge relief when we spot him limping ahead. He's made it even less far than I thought and it's obvious he is carrying some kind of an injury that is hampering his progress.

'Cole, wait! We need to talk!' Kim says and, to my surprise, Cole actually stops and faces us rather than carrying on in vain to get away from us.

'I have nothing to say to you two,' he tells us. 'I just want to go home.'

'That's okay. We'll take you home. But we need to talk about what just happened.'

'You mean you killing someone?'

Hearing it like that shuts Kim up, but I take over.

'Cole, we understand we have a lot to talk about and there's so much we're sorry for. But right now, this is bigger than that. We're going to have to call the police and when we do, we need to know that you won't say anything stupid.'

'I won't. I'll tell the truth.'

'That's the problem,' I say.

'So you want me to lie?'

It sounds even harsher when put like that, but that's what we're asking him to do.

Kim looks terrified, so I have to take charge, trying to do what might be the best thing we can do in the circumstances.

'I know this is hard to say because it's still so raw, but us three are family,' I tell both Cole and Kim. 'That means we have to stick together. Protect each other. To do that, we can't tell the police that Lewis lowered his gun before he got shot, otherwise your mum will go to prison for murder.'

I'm expecting a pause while the gravity of what I have said sinks in for Cole, but I don't get it.

'But it's a lie!' he says, shocked we would even consider such a thing.

'I know it is, but we have to consider what's best for all of us and your mum going to prison for several years is not what's best. So maybe it's better to tell them something else. It won't change Lewis being gone. We can't bring him back now. No matter what. The fact is that Lewis was pointing a gun at us, and your mum was only trying to save us.'

'But it's not fair! He wasn't going to kill anybody, and he shouldn't be remembered as if he was!'

Cole has a good, strong point and it's admirable that he is so passionately trying to defend Lewis's honour and preserve the memory of him so that he isn't just seen as some crazy guy who was about to go on a murderous spree before being cut down at the last second.

'But what else can we do?' Kim cries. 'I can't go to prison. And I can't lose you!'

Both Kim and Cole look afraid and desperate now, so it feels like it's on me to sort this mess out. But I'm not sure how I could if we can't agree on this. That is until I have an idea.

'Lewis told me that he was having problems with his business today,' I confess. 'And he was drinking heavily before he pulled out the gun. What if we tell the police that he killed himself?'

That elicits an awkward silence between us before the debating quickly starts again.

'But he didn't kill himself!' Cole cries.

'Yes, I know that, but think about it. What good is it going to do your mother if she tells them she killed him, in self-defence or not? They might believe her but they might not and then she'll go to prison. Do you want that, Cole?'

Kim looks afraid at the prospect of prison, but Cole looks just as scared.

'No,' he admits, which is a huge relief because it feels like we might be getting somewhere now.

'Okay, then we need to make sure there's no chance of that,' I carry on. 'I think the best way of doing that is telling them that Lewis went for a walk by himself and hasn't come back. We can just call the police and tell them he is missing, and they'll come up here to look for him. When they find him, it'll look like he killed himself.'

'But I shot him in the chest, not the head,' Kim reminds me.

'It doesn't matter. People can kill themselves that way too.'

'But it's a lie,' Cole mumbles, and I worry we might lose him here again.

'Look, Lewis was angry, confused, not to mention very

drunk. Who knows what he would have done,' I say, reminding him of the danger we were just in. 'He might have raised his gun again a second later and fired and who knows where he would have stopped.'

I'm trying to insinuate that Cole could have been one of his targets, but the teenager isn't buying it.

'No, he said he wasn't going to hurt me.'

'That doesn't mean he wouldn't have,' I remind him. 'He had lost control of himself. He could have hurt any of us. What if he had shot your mother too? And what if he had gone back to the cabin and hurt Nicola or Emily?'

'No, he wouldn't have done that,' Cole says defiantly, but I can tell he's not entirely convinced about that after seeing how deranged Lewis was before he died.

'We are just trying to do what is best to keep all of us safe,' I say. 'Kim and I love you. We really do. But things will be harder if Kim goes to prison, so we need to make sure we don't leave it up to the police to decide for us, okay?'

Cole goes quiet then, but I can tell he is coming around to my way of thinking and, after several more minutes of convincing him, he very reluctantly agrees to go along with the story. But he only does so nonverbally, not saying anything, simply nodding his head in a very hesitant and weary fashion.

'Lewis went for a walk. Lewis never came back. That's all we know. Okay?' I say, spelling it out to make it clear what we need to say when asked.

'What about the guns?' Kim wants to know. 'The one nearest to Lewis's body didn't fire but if he killed himself then we need to swap it with the one I used.'

'Don't worry about that, I can swap them,' I say. 'But first, let's get back to the cabin. The mechanic will be out to fix the car anytime now and it'll be better for our story if we're all there when he arrives. That way it looks like Lewis really has gone off on his own.'

That makes sense so we start walking. But there's another reason why I need to get back to the cabin before I go and deal with the guns back behind me in the forest.

I need to talk to Nicola.

Urgently.

TWENTY-SEVEN

NICOLA

Hearing the gunshot was one thing but finding out that two guns were now in play was another. Kim must have taken the second gun but was she the one who fired? Or was it Lewis? I have no idea and I'll only get some answers when people start coming back to this cabin. But, so far, nobody has appeared out of the forest and it's still just Emily and I cowering in this holiday house and feeling terrified about what might happen next.

'I want to go home,' Emily says again, repeating the same thing she has been telling me for much of the last thirty minutes since I discovered both guns were gone now. That's how long we've been stressing over this situation, and the longer it goes on, the more I fear something truly awful has happened out amongst those trees.

I can feel it in my bones.

Somebody is dead.

But who?

'I want to go and find Daddy,' Emily tells me, the second thing she has been saying to go along with her desire to go home.

'He'll be back soon,' I say, starting to repeat myself now but what else can I do? Be honest and say that Daddy might never be coming back because he might just have been shot?

'Wait here,' I tell Emily, deciding that I am going to leave her in the ensuite, where we have been hiding for the last half hour, so I can go downstairs and have another look outside.

Emily isn't happy about me leaving her, but I tell her I'll be back as quickly as I can before I go, closing the bathroom door behind me and instructing Emily to only open it again if I'm the one who wants to get in.

The cabin is eerily quiet as I creep around it, but the gunshot is still ringing in my ears as I reach the front doors and look through the glass. If I could see anybody, I'd choose to see Ryan emerging from the trees, because even though he has broken my heart, I would at least be relieved to see he was okay, for Emily's sake if no one else's. I'd also know that he could protect us from whatever danger might still possibly be lurking out there in the trees and that would be something too. But I don't see him or anybody else yet.

Wherever they all are, they must still be making their way back.

The gunshot seemed relatively close but it's hard to tell. It could have just echoed and maybe it was actually miles away. If it was then whoever is alive might not get back here for hours yet. The thought that Emily and I might still be on our own here when darkness falls hours from now is a troubling one, but I have to stay positive.

And then I see movement in the trees.

The flash of grey that catches my attention might be a deer but then I see that's it not the fur of an animal and is actually the colour of the jeans worn by Cole. The teenager is here, and he's followed by Kim and Ryan.

But there's just the three of them.

Where's Lewis?

I'm wary of any of them carrying a gun but I don't see any weapon in their hands, which is why I'm confident enough to stay standing by the front door as they approach it. When the door opens, Cole quickly hurries past me and heads upstairs, and even though I ask him what just happened out there, he doesn't answer me. He soon disappears and I hear a door slam. Kim and Ryan are still here so they can give me some answers.

'What's happened? Where's Lewis?'

I expect an immediate answer, but I don't get one. Instead, Kim and Ryan just look at each other awkwardly.

'What is going on? I heard a gunshot? Is Lewis okay?'

'Listen, we need to talk,' Ryan starts.

'Yes, we do, so talk!'

I don't like how my husband is looking at me. It's as if he is afraid. But of what?

'Lewis had a gun,' he begins.

'Yes, I know that. There were two guns. I'm guessing you had the other one.'

I look at Kim then, but she is staying quiet.

'Well, while we were out walking, Lewis confessed a few things. He told me his business was struggling. Said he has money problems.'

I wasn't expecting that, but I keep listening.

'He was quite distressed. He started drinking heavily from a whiskey bottle. He was even giving some to Cole. He was really in a bad way.'

'So where is he now?'

Ryan hesitates to answer.

'Ryan! Talk to me. For once in your life, tell me the truth!'

I'm trying to provoke a response from my husband, but in the end it's Kim who answers me. 'He's dead!'

The words were spoken loud and clear and suddenly the cabin is silent again.

'What?'

Kim nods her head, so I look to Ryan.

'It's true,' he confirms.

'What do you mean he's dead? How did he die?'

More hesitation.

'How did he die?' I ask again.

'He shot himself,' Ryan tells me.

'No,' I say, my hands going to my mouth, and I stagger backwards a little.

'He was in a really bad way,' Ryan goes on. 'He said everything was getting on top of him and then he just pulled the trigger.'

'I don't believe it. He wouldn't do that.'

Kim has tears in her eyes, but Ryan is staring blankly back at me.

'It wasn't just about the business,' he admits. 'It was about the other thing too. The thing you've just found out about.'

I know exactly what he means, but there's something in the way Ryan says it that sounds so cold. *The thing you've just found out about.* As if it's just another problem Lewis had to deal with, nothing major, just one of life's regular issues. That's one way to sum up cheating and lying about a child's father.

'Lewis knew too?' I ask, and Ryan nods.

My head is swimming with so many questions and while Ryan keeps talking, explaining what happened and how it's important this gets discussed before the mechanic arrives to fix the car, I ignore him and take a seat on the sofa before holding my head in my hands.

Lewis is dead. That poor man. And his decision had something to do with what Ryan and Kim did.

'This is on you two,' I say to them both. 'His blood is on your hands.'

Neither Ryan nor Kim say anything in response, perhaps rather wisely because if they tried in any way to defend themselves then I will explode at them and give them plenty more home truths. But with the pair quiet, my thoughts turn to the two youngsters upstairs. I know Emily is safe for now because I only left her a moment ago. But what about Cole? How is he handling things?

'Was Cole there when it happened?' I ask. 'Did he see it?'

'Yes,' Kim replies grimly before Ryan cuts in.

'He'd tried to run away before. He was upset about...'

Neither finishes their sentences, and I take a guess at what they were going to say.

'Upset about finding out he had been lied to about who his real dad was?'

Once again, neither of them dignifies that with a response.

'So he knows Lewis is dead, right?' I ask, and Kim nods to confirm.

'The poor kid,' I say. 'Somebody better go and check on him.'

'I will do in a minute,' Kim replies, but then she looks at Ryan as if she is waiting for him to sort something out before she leaves.

'What is it?' I ask, fearful of what more there could be to this horrendous set of circumstances we find ourselves in.

Ryan takes a seat on the sofa beside me but knows better than to try and touch me. Instead, he just starts talking.

'Considering everything that has happened between us all, and how the police might look at things when they get here, we were thinking it might be best if we just tell them Lewis went for a walk and never came back.'

It takes me a second to process what Ryan has just said, but when I do I realise he wants me to lie.

'What? Why wouldn't you just tell them the truth?'

'Because they might not believe us,' he says. 'If we tell them that Kim and I were with Lewis when he died then they might think we had something to do with it, especially if they find out about Cole and what happened in the past between us.'

I can't believe this. Is he serious? Instead of apologising for what he did with Kim, he is asking me to do them both a favour?

'You want me to help you two?' I ask, my voice dripping with disdain.

'No, not help us. Not exactly. Just avoid this horrible situation dragging out any longer than it needs to. If we tell the police Lewis went for a walk then they'll find him and think he just turned a gun on himself. But if we say we were all there then it complicates things.'

'But it doesn't matter if it's the truth!' I cry. 'Why lie if you don't need to?'

And then I figure it out.

These pair of liars are lying about something else.

'What are you not telling me?' I ask them, fearful of things getting even worse.

'Nothing,' Ryan pretends but now I know him to be a liar, it's as if I can't believe a word that comes out of his mouth any more.

'Tell me!' I cry. 'There's something else, isn't there? So what is it?'

I am hardly expecting my husband to be honest and spill the beans but, in the end, I don't need him to because Kim goes to speak first.

'Lewis didn't kill himself,' she says and as I turn to look at her, I can tell she isn't finished talking. But then Ryan speaks next.

'I did.'

'What?'

Now I'm staring at Ryan again and he's nodding his head slowly.

'Lewis pulled a gun on me, but Kim got there to interrupt him. When she did, I grabbed her gun and shot Lewis.'

This all sounds crazy, but Kim isn't disputing it so maybe it is true.

'It was self-defence,' Ryan tells me. 'But I can't tell the police that. If they don't believe me then I go to prison and what will that do to this family? Even if you can't forgive me for what I've done, Emily doesn't deserve to grow up without a father.'

I can't believe it. Is he really going there? Using Emily to try and hold together this pathetic excuse for a family now? It seems like it, or maybe he is just using her so that I go along with his desire for me to tell the police that Lewis just wandered off for a walk and never came back.

'I don't know,' I say, leaving the sofa and needing to put some space between myself and him.

'Please, Nicola. Just tell the police Lewis went for a walk and that's all we need. They'll believe he killed himself and that will be the end of it. If not for me then for Emily.'

'Stop talking about her!' I cry, but that just confirms that he knows my weak spot and isn't afraid to exploit it.

'Okay, I'm sorry,' he tells me, and it looks as though he is going to give me a little space now, so I tell him what my next move is.

'I just need some time to think about all of this,' I say, planning to go upstairs and be with my daughter for a moment.

'We don't have time,' Kim suddenly says as she looks out of the window. 'The mechanic is here.'

The arrival of the person we have been waiting for ever since Cole flattened the battery on the car should have been a welcome one. But not now. All it means is that I have a matter of seconds to decide what to do next, and as I see the van parking outside the cabin, I'm still not sure what that will be.

TWENTY-EIGHT

RYAN

Kim and I have decided to be the ones to go out and deal with the arrival of the mechanic. Nicola is still processing what we've just told her so it's better if she stays inside, out of sight. There's still a lot for us to discuss when we go back in, but for now, all I care about is assisting the man who has turned up here to help us get our car roadworthy again.

'Hey,' I say as I wave to the guy getting out of the large white van. 'Thanks for coming so quickly.'

'You're lucky it's not the middle of winter. You'd have been stuck for days if it was snowing,' the fifty-something man with wiry white hair and a sizeable gut tells me. 'Six months ago, I had to rescue a couple who had got stuck in a car park near Ben Nevis. It shouldn't have been too remote, but they'd gone there in the middle of a snowstorm and there was no one else around. I'm surprised they hadn't frozen to death. Tourists, hey.'

I'm not sure if he's having a dig at me with that tourist remark but I just smile and pretend he isn't.

'So, you must be Lewis,' he says. 'I'm Hamish.'

He goes to shake my hand then, but I realise I have to correct him before we go any further.

'Oh, no. I'm not Lewis. I'm Ryan. Lewis was the one who called you earlier.'

'So where is he then?'

I glance nervously at Kim, who has so far been lingering behind me during this exchange but now she steps to the forefront.

'He's still not back yet,' she tells Hamish. 'He had to go quite a way to get a phone signal.'

'I imagine he did,' Hamish replies, brushing off what look like breadcrumbs from his work uniform. 'The main road would have been the best bet for him. But I didn't see him down there when I drove up.'

'He'll be in the middle of the forest somewhere now,' I say when Kim has failed to answer quickly enough. 'Walking back. Takes a few hours, I suppose.'

'And no one bothered to go with him?'

Hamish has rather a lot of questions, all of which are only increasing the awkwardness for those of us having to answer them.

'Erm, I offered. But he said he wanted to go alone. I think he needed some space.'

'Well, he'll get plenty of that out here. But why did he need it?'

'Erm...'

I don't know what to say to that, but Kim comes to my rescue this time.

'He's been under some pressure lately. Work stuff. He said he fancied a long walk and was happy to go by himself.'

Hamish stares at us both for what feels like long enough for him to figure out we're lying to him but then he just shrugs and turns his attentions to the car beside us.

'So you've got yourselves a flat battery, have you? How did that happen?'

Kim explains about Cole and the mistake he made leaving the key in the ignition earlier, and Hamish chuckles to himself.

'Ahh, the old teenage son story. You'd be surprised how much that happens. Funny, isn't it. They all say they can't wait to drive but the first time they get behind a wheel, they only end up draining the car of all its power. But not my kids. I've made sure to teach them not to do that before it happens.'

I suspect that might be another dig at us and how none of us bothered to tell Cole that leaving the key in the ignition without the engine on could cause problems, and if I didn't know any better, I'd say Hamish isn't exactly thrilled to be here today. I'm not exactly thrilled to have him either with everything else that is going on, so I do my best to speed this thing up.

'How long do you think it will take to get it going again?' I ask, but that question only seems to slow Hamish down more.

'It'll take as long as it takes,' he replies in the annoying manner of a person who knows he is needed and thus has all the power.

After examining the stricken car for himself, he returns to his own vehicle and begins to take out some tools for his job including charging cables, and while he's busy with that, Kim and I move away from him so we can talk quietly.

'Why did he ask about Lewis?' Kim wants to know, the paranoia seemingly pouring out of her.

'Because Lewis was the one who phoned him. That's all.'

'What if he knows something's happened to him?'

'How would he know that?'

'He might be able to tell that we're lying.'

'No, he can't. He's just here to fix the car. He doesn't care about anything else.'

I keep watching Hamish as he clamps one end of his cables to our dead battery before he attaches the other end to the battery in his van. He's not exactly working quickly but at least he's working, and with a bit of luck, the car battery will be working soon as well. But until then, Kim is still letting me know how anxious she is.

'We should have just told him the truth,' she says.

'Are you crazy? He came here to fix a car, not be told about a dead body.'

'I know, but we've lied now and it's too late to go back.'

'So we don't go back. We just stick to our plan.'

'Which is?'

'We get the car fixed and I'll go back to Lewis and swap the guns. While I'm doing that, you will have driven to the main road and you will call the police and say you're worried because your husband hasn't returned from his trip into the forest.'

'Why do I have to be the one to speak to the police?'

'Because he's your husband.'

I really shouldn't have to be explaining this to Kim and I wish I didn't have to, especially not with a grumpy Scottish stranger so close to us. Hamish is leaning against his van and keeps glancing at his watch every few minutes, presumably checking how long the charging cables have been doing their job. From my limited knowledge of things like this, I know it shouldn't take too long to get some charge into the battery. In the meantime, Kim asks me more questions.

'Why the hell did you tell Nicola that you shot Lewis?'

'Because she'd be more willing to protect me from the police than you.'

I thought that was obvious and Kim can't argue with that.

'I knew you were going to tell her what happened,' I go on. 'So I interrupted you and edited the story. Otherwise, there was no way Nicola would have helped lie to the police for us. But now she thinks I shot Lewis, she will lie because she won't want me going to prison, not when we have Emily to think about.'

Of course I can't know that for sure. It's just a calculated gamble, yet another in what is becoming a long line of calculated gambles that started when I slept with Kim and kept my secret hidden. I suppose they had always paid off. *Until today.*

We're interrupted then when Hamish gives us a shout and a thumbs up not long after.

'You should be able to start the engine now,' he says. 'Give it a go.'

I look to Kim, but she tells me she doesn't have the keys and there's a brief, unspoken moment of panic between us as we both worry that the keys might be in Lewis's pockets. But, thankfully, they are on the kitchen counter in the cabin and, once Kim has them, she gets behind the wheel and tries the engine.

It starts, though only just, and Hamish tells us we'll need to drive it for at least fifteen minutes now to keep charging the battery.

I tell him that's fine, anything to get him on his way again, and as he tidies up his work tools, I think about how we have just overcome the first obstacle. Now we have a working car again, things seem a little brighter. Not that Kim looks any happier about things. She looks positively pale behind the wheel and I'm worried that she might not be able to make it to the main road and call the police, but it's imperative that she does.

'Okay, so who's signing for this?' Hamish asks as he produces a sheet of paper.

I gesture to Kim, and she scribbles her signature on the form before Hamish asks her about payment.

'My husband would usually deal with that,' she mumbles, but I swoop in and say I'm happy to sort it out in his absence.

'We can send you an invoice,' Hamish tells us. 'As long as you've paid within fourteen days then there's no problems. But if not, well, then there will be a problem.'

If he's joking then he's not done a very good job of delivering the punchline or judging his audience because neither

Kim nor I laugh. We just watch the burly mechanic amble back to his van, and after giving us a dismissive wave, he starts his engine and reverses away from the cabin.

As the van disappears down the track in the direction of the main road, I wonder if the driver of it will give any more thought to us today or if we were just another in a long list of irritating tourists he has to rescue in his line of work. Hopefully it's the latter because the less he thinks about us and how Lewis wasn't around when he turned up, the better. But at least if he is questioned by the police at a later date then our story about Lewis not being back yet will match what we tell them.

But we've got enough on our plate without worrying about a mechanic.

Soon enough, it'll be time to worry about the police.

TWENTY-NINE

NICOLA

I was glad the mechanic turned up at the cabin and not just because it means the car is going to be finally fixed. It's because it gave me a break from Ryan and Kim. With the pair of them going outside, I was left with some time to think to myself, and after trying to process all that they told me, I'm still not sure I believe it.

Ryan shot Lewis? Is that what actually happened? The thought of my husband holding a gun let alone firing it and hitting another human being is hard enough to wrap my head around. Was it really in self-defence? Was Lewis really going to shoot them if they hadn't shot first? If so then I guess Ryan had no choice but still, killing someone is a terrible thing to have to do, and is the man I married really capable of doing it?

I'm troubled by the fact that Kim and Ryan initially tried to make me believe that Lewis killed himself. If they were telling me the truth that it was really self-defence then why the need for the charade? Is it because they were covering something up or is it just because they thought it was plausible that Lewis could have pulled the trigger on himself?

The evidence for him doing such a devastating thing is

certainly there if he was struggling with his business. But it's the revelation about him not being Cole's father that could have been the thing that tipped him over the edge, and while I would have previously thought there was no way he could have left this world voluntary knowing that he would be leaving his child behind in the process, him turning out to not be a father after all removes that potential barrier.

So maybe I could have believed that Lewis did do it. But now it turns out he didn't and having been told two versions of events, is it any wonder I'm left feeling confused?

Even though I've now apparently been told the truth, there's still something about this that doesn't sit right with me, and I know it's because Ryan and Kim have lied before. What's stopping them again? Perhaps another secret, one even darker than the secret they have kept for so long about Cole.

Cole.

He's the key to all of this because he was out in the forest with them. I could ask him what happened and even if he isn't forthcoming with the answer, I should be able to get a better idea of whether there is more to this than I have been told.

I know the teenager is still hiding upstairs somewhere so I go up, but before I find Cole, I check on Emily. Bless her, she is still doing what I told her to do when I last left her, which is remain in the ensuite and only open the door if I tell her that it's me outside it.

When I see my little girl, she has tears in her eyes, but I hug her tightly and tell her that everything is going to be okay.

'What about Daddy?' she wants to know.

'He's back now and he's safe.'

Only at that news does she relax and it's clear that her love for Ryan is as strong as ever. It's a shame the same can't be said of my feelings for him.

'I need to go and talk to Cole for a minute, but you can go and wait for me in your bedroom if you'd like,' I say to Emily, and she is happy enough with that, so I take her to her room and get her settled on her bed with her book.

'I'll be right back,' I tell her before leaving and going into Cole's room, but when I get there, I find there is no sign of him.

'Cole?' I call out, but I get no response from any other room.

After a little more exploring, I find the bathroom door is locked and figure he must be in there, so I knock gently on the door and ask him if he's okay. But again, I get no response.

'Cole, I'm really sorry about what has happened, and I know you must be suffering right now,' I tell him, keeping my voice as low as I can so Emily won't hear me. 'I understand you just want to be alone, but I need to ask you something. I need to know what happened in the forest.'

I get no response and I wonder if it's because Cole is afraid of saying anything if he thinks his mum is nearby.

'Your mum is outside with the mechanic,' I tell him. 'And Ryan is too. It's just me out here but they'll be back in soon. So if there's anything you want to tell me before they get here then you can do it now.'

I'm hoping to hear the sound of the door unlocking or at least a few words back. But all I get is more silence and now I'm starting to worry that Cole might have hurt himself in there.

'Cole, just make a noise to let me know that you're okay,' I say, my voice more urgent because I'm worried this day might be getting even worse before it's over with. 'I'm worried about you. Just let me know you're okay and I'll leave you alone.'

I wait impatiently for some sign from the bathroom that the teenager is safe and well and, eventually, I get it.

'Go away,' comes the quiet, sorry response, and at least I don't have to worry any more about him being hurt. But I'm still worried about getting to the truth, so now that he's talking to me I try my luck again.

'Can you just tell me what happened in the forest? Ryan and Kim have told me, but I want to ask you too. Is that okay?'

I'm hopeful but Cole is quiet again now and it seems I'm pushing my luck with him.

I hear the sound of two engines outside the cabin then and figure the car must be working again, so that means Kim and Ryan will be back in here any minute. I'm running out of time to get any answers out of Cole, and I tell him that one more time to see if he will open up to me. But he doesn't and when I hear somebody re-entering the cabin downstairs, I figure it's best to leave the bathroom for now.

'The car is fixed,' Ryan tells me when I see him. 'It just needs to be driven for a little while to fully charge the battery, so Kim has taken it out.'

I don't say anything because it's hard to get too excited about the car being mended when the person who drove it here is now dead.

'You need to phone the police,' I tell Ryan after he's poured himself a large glass of water and gulped down half of it.

'Kim's going to call them from the main road. But it's too early yet. We need a little more time to pass before we can report him missing.'

'Or just tell them that he's already dead and that you were there when it happened.'

Ryan lowers his glass and he's either finished quenching his thirst or he doesn't like what I've just suggested.

'We talked about this. We decided it would be best if we just told the police that Lewis didn't come back.'

'Best for who?'

'For all of us.'

'What do you mean all of us? What does this have to do with me or Emily?'

'I told you. We don't want the police asking too many questions. If they know I was there when Lewis died then they might suspect me.'

'What have you got to worry about if you didn't do anything wrong?'

'But I did do something wrong, didn't I?' Ryan admits. 'I lied to you. I slept with Kim. We conceived Cole. And we're the reason Lewis is dead. We destroyed that man's life and that's something both of us will have to live with forever. But why make it any worse? Why subject ourselves to having to hope the police believe us when we say it was self-defence rather than just say we weren't even with him when it happened?'

'I just don't think lying is a good idea.'

'It doesn't change the facts. Lewis is still dead, whatever we say. But this way, no one else might get in any trouble.'

Even though what he did with Kim all those years ago tells me my husband can be a very selfish man, I can see now that that selfishness knows no bounds and he'd still rather lie, even to the police, if it's in his best interests.

'At least you're good at it,' I tell him, shaking my head.

'Good at what?'

'Lying.'

Ryan knows me well enough to see that even if I go along with all of this, things are never going to be the same between me and him. But right now, maybe he cares less about that and more about covering up the mess with Lewis.

'Where's Emily?' he asks me.

'In her room.'

'Is she okay?'

'What do you care?'

'Of course I care. She's my daughter.'

'You haven't asked about your other child yet.'

I hope that makes Ryan feel as uncomfortable as it should do.

'He's locked himself in the bathroom if you're interested,' I say flippantly. 'Refuses to come out or talk to me. Just wants to be left alone. I guess he's scarred for life now with whatever he saw out there, so well done on a great parenting job.'

'Nicola, please. Don't be like this.'

'How do you want me to be? If I haven't made it clear yet, then let me make it clear now. When all of this is over, so are we. You hear me? We're finished and don't even bother trying to get custody of Emily because after what you have done to this family, there's little chance of that.'

Ryan is hurt but that only makes me want to keep going.

'It's not just what you've done to me,' I say. 'Or Emily. It's that poor boy up there. He must be so confused and not know who to believe any more.'

'I'll go and talk to him.'

'Didn't you hear me? I just said he wants to be left alone.'

'Fine. I don't have time for this. I need to go back to Lewis.'

'Why? I thought we were just calling the police and letting them find him.'

'There's two guns with his body. We need to take one otherwise the police will think someone else was on the scene.'

I don't like the thought of Ryan returning to the scene any more than I do of him handling a gun, but if we are to tell the police that Lewis killed himself then it would be better if there was only one gun there, I suppose. That means Ryan is going to have to leave me again, something I'm starting to get used to.

'Fine. Do what you have to do,' I tell him. 'Just keep me, Emily and Cole out of it.'

THIRTY

RYAN

I'm ten minutes into my hurried trek back to Lewis's body when I realise finding it again might not be as easy as I thought. It's one thing to be covering plenty of ground as I run as fast as I can through here, but as well as having to dodge sharp branches and trip hazards, the light is fading a little overhead as the sun begins its descent in the sky and thanks to all the stress of the situation earlier, I'm not sure I took enough care in noting exactly where I need to go to get back there. I should have been looking for memorable points along the route, like an unusually shaped tree or how many paces the clearing was from the track. Instead, I'm now left trying to remember the way and that's not easy, not only because my memory has never been the sharpest. It's because I've got so much to worry about on route and the police aren't even the half of it.

I'm terrified that Cole hates me now and will never want to see me again. Not only did he find out that I'd been lying to him but then he saw the man who has raised him all his life die and knows I'm pretty much the reason for it. Could I really blame Cole if he never wanted to speak to me ever again? I can't but I pray that's not how he feels because I need my son in my life, however limited that access might be.

I've managed to get through these last fifteen years with seeing him sporadically and under the guise of being a family friend but that was hard enough. Not seeing him at all would tear me apart, and now he knows I'm his real father, I want nothing more than to have a good relationship with him. But that remains to be seen and is probably asking for far too much at this stage. He'll need time, probably a lot of it, before he can consider letting me in. I'm willing to give him all the space he needs. Just as long as when he's ready, the door is open for me to be there for him whenever he might need me in the future.

With Lewis dead, Cole has lost the only father figure he had and at a crucial stage of his life. He's becoming a man and will have to do battle with all that entails and that's not easy at the best of times. But it'll be even harder without a strong male influence around, so I'm hoping he will realise that and allow me to be the father I should always have been to him.

Just like with Cole, my relationship with Kim going forward is likely to prove to be a difficult one. Where do we stand now? Her husband is dead and I'm doing all I can to keep her from getting in trouble with the law for that. If we're successful in passing this off as suicide then it will mean that the pair of us are bound together forever in our lie. Then again, we've been bound together by a lie for a long time already, so what's one more to add to the equation?

There's no denying that Kim and I have been close and, whatever we do, it seems we can't break free of each other. I've never harboured hopes of a real, romantic relationship with her, even after the night we spent together, but what about how she feels? With Lewis out of the picture, is there a chance that she starts to entertain thoughts of the pair of us trying to reignite that spark we once had? But it doesn't matter if she does because I'm only interested in Nicola.

Nicola. My amazing wife. The woman who does not deserve any of this. God, I've been awful to her and turned her world upside down. She must hate me so much and the worst thing is that she would be incredibly justified in feeling that way. Even I hate me right now. But will that hate ever subside? Will she be able to find it in her heart to forgive me? I hope so. If not, my future only gets even more uncertain.

Who wants to start again and at my age, with my baggage? I'm a walking disaster.

And right now, I don't even know if I'm walking in the right direction.

I thought I was back on the right track but I'm suddenly not so sure again when I come to a clearing in the trees that I don't recognise. The fear that I'll not be able to relocate Lewis and sort the gun situation out causes me to feel nauseous, because if I can't then what Kim will very shortly be telling the police will not make sense. I can't contact her because I have no signal on my phone, though it won't be long until she has a signal on hers and makes the important call.

Come on, Ryan. Concentrate. You can do this.

Scratch that.

You have to do this.

I take a moment to try and get my bearings again before forging on through the trees, and I soon start to feel better when I pass through what feels like a familiar part of the forest. This is more like it. This is the right way but I still have some distance to cover.

I wish I'd taken more care to sort the guns out at the time, but like Kim and Cole I was in shock over what had happened. I also had to make sure that I was with them when they got back to the cabin and saw Nicola, so there was little chance of me hanging around in the forest. I'll certainly be glad to see the back of this place soon, and from now on the only trees I want to look at are the ones at the bottom of my back garden.

After half an hour of a desperate combination of running, jogging and powerwalking, the last occurring when the terrain was too unforgiving to do anything faster, I see the clearing that I need up ahead. Only then do I slow down to a walk and that's because I have to prepare myself for the sight that I'm about to witness for the second time.

Just as I remember it, Lewis's body is gruesome and sobering. The same amount of blood. The same lifeless expression behind the eyes. And the same knowledge that the only reason this man is dead is because of what I did with his wife all those years ago.

I decide it's best to just do what I need to do as quickly as possible and get out of here before I'm overwhelmed with guilt, shame or just plain nausea, so I find the gun that Kim fired and carefully pick it up, using the sleeve of my jacket so as to not get any fingerprints on it. I also make sure to wipe off Kim's prints before I place it in the hand of Lewis, a torturous job and not just because it's hard to be so close to a dead man. Once the gun has been touched by him, I lay it down beside his body before picking up the one Lewis originally had because that's the one that needs to come back to the cabin with me.

Satisfied that this scene now looks more like one in which a man killed himself rather than was shot by another person, I figure all that is left to do now is get out of here. But then I notice Lewis's rucksack lying on the ground near his body and I can't resist taking a look inside it, just in case there might be anything in there that could still mess up this whole thing for me. A note from beyond the grave or something like that, some kind of insurance policy that Lewis put in place in case any harm came to him. All I find in there are a few snacks and his wallet, one that contains a photo of him, Kim and Cole in happier times.

I wish I'd never seen it almost as soon as I lay my eyes on it because I know it's an image that is going to haunt me for the rest of my life. A once happy man surrounded by love, only for the truth to come out and send him on a collision course with this clearing in the forest at this time and with these deadly results.

I leave his belongings as they are in the backpack and make my way back, the gun by my side as I walk through the forest. I'm moving much slower than when I came through this way not so long ago, as if my legs are weighed down by some invisible and heavy force, but I know it's just more guilt manifesting itself in a slightly different way. I also know my slow movements reflect my reluctance to get back to the cabin too quickly, because there's only more death stares from Nicola waiting for me there.

It occurs to me that this silent, solitary march of mine through the forest might not be the last time I'm so lonely for a while. I expect to be very lonely when we make it back to Preston and Nicola tells me to pack up my things and leave our home. Where will I go? A hotel is my best bet if I want to keep this quiet from the rest of my family and friends, but that will only work for so long. They'll find out eventually, from Nicola if not from me, so there's no point burning through cash in some bed and breakfast if I could stay on a mate's sofa for much cheaper. But will any of them let me? They're all married with kids of their own. Would they want me taking up space in their loving homes after what I've done? Or worse, would they tell me I've let them down and that it's best if I sort this out on my own?

For a brief moment, I'm almost a little envious that Lewis doesn't have to deal with all of this. At least his problems are over now. But mine aren't. I'm right in the middle of them all.

And things are about to get a hell of a lot worse.

THIRTY-ONE

NICOLA

With Kim out in the car and Ryan doing whatever he needs to do in the forest, I'm once again alone with just Emily and Cole in the cabin. I've checked on my daughter one more time, as well as tried to speak to the teenager behind the locked bathroom door too, but other than that, not much has changed. I'm still anxious, confused and feeling like I'll never really know what happened out amongst those trees earlier.

And then I hear the bathroom door unlock.

I realise Cole must finally be ready to come out, so I step away from the door and give him as much space as he needs. The last thing I want is for him to feel like I'm crowding him and to disappear back inside, so I try to prove that I'll keep my distance and take things as quickly or as slowly as he wants to.

When I see him, I can tell that he has been crying because his eyes are stained red and his cheeks are blotchy, a result of him wiping them several times while he was in there. He does his best to disguise this by keeping his head bowed but it's obvious and, along with the sniffling coming from the troubled teenager, I can see he is in quite a bad way.

It's horrible to see someone so young so upset, as if they

don't deserve to feel such a way yet, because they're only just embarking on this journey called life and they should still easily be in the innocent, carefree stage. It's only when they reach adulthood that things should, and often do, become trickier. But Cole is suffering right now, right here in front of me, and with the other adults not currently here I feel like I'm the only one who can help him.

Will he let me?

I take him leaving the bathroom as a good sign that he might finally be ready to talk, so I cautiously try one more time to get him to open up to me.

'Can I get you a drink or anything?' I ask him, afraid he might just rush past me and disappear into his bedroom. But he doesn't. He just stays standing before me like someone who doesn't know what to do with themselves. And then I just go for it, rushing towards him and giving him a hug before I can change my mind about doing it or he can have the time to get away from me.

Feeling his exhausted, weak and fragile body pressed up against mine only confirms to me how broken he is, but it's a relief when he doesn't pull away. Instead, he just lets me squeeze him and tell him everything is going to be okay before he lets his tears flow, openly this time instead of behind closed doors. As he is sobbing into my left shoulder, I stroke Cole's hair and give him as long as he needs to calm down again and, eventually, he lifts his head up and wipes his snotty nose.

Then he says something that tells me exactly how he feels about Kim and Ryan at this moment in time.

'Where are *they*?' he asks.

His tone of voice suggests he is asking not because he wants to see them but because he wants to make sure they aren't around.

'They're not here. Kim's out in the car and Ryan's in the forest.'

'Doing what?'

'Your mum's going to phone the police and Ryan is...'

Even though I know what he's doing, I stop short of saying it out loud because, somehow, I don't think Cole would like to be reminded of Lewis's dead body and the guns lying beside it.

'I know it doesn't seem like it now, but everything is going to be okay,' I tell Cole then, hoping I sound more convincing than it feels coming out. 'I know you've been lied to. I have too. But take some comfort in knowing that the truth always comes out. We're on the side of honesty, so we'll always be okay.'

I just want to make Cole feel even slightly better than he currently does, but it doesn't work because it seems my comment about truth and honesty has him riled up.

'How can I be honest when I'm surrounded by liars?' he asks me, which is far too deep of a question for a fifteen-year-old kid to be asking.

'I'm not lying to you,' I try, but it's clear that's not what he means.

'My parents are.'

'Kim and Ryan?'

'Yeah.'

'But you know the truth now. About what happened between them.'

I expect that's what he's talking about, but he shakes his head then.

'No, that's not what I mean.'

'Then what?'

'What did they tell you about what happened out there?'

I realise he means out in the forest with Lewis, and while I don't really want to go over it, wary of traumatising the youngster any more than he already is, he has asked me the question.

'They said Lewis had a gun and was going to shoot at Kim or Ryan. But Ryan grabbed the second gun and shot him before he could.'

I decide not to mention the suicide story because that might only confuse Cole more, but I'm wondering if they tried to get him to tell that original story too. But it seems Cole knows something else happened.

A third version of events.

'No, they're lying again,' he says.

'In what way?'

'It wasn't Ryan who shot Lewis. It was Mum.'

If that's true then it means Ryan has lied to me again. But why? If he has taken the blame for the shooting over Kim then I can only think that he is trying to protect her. But from what?

'Dad wasn't going to shoot,' Cole says, still referring to Lewis as his father even though he knows that's not technically true, which speaks volumes about how he feels about the man who really is his dad.

'But he had a gun,' I say, 'and he knew that Ryan and Kim had lied to him. He wanted revenge.'

'Maybe he did at the start, but he changed his mind. He lowered his gun. I saw him do it. But Mum still shot him.'

I can't believe what I've just heard, but it does make sense why Ryan would want to cover this up and why he's now out in the forest doing just that. The pair of them have something to hide. If what Cole is saying is true, they weren't acting to save themselves.

They shot a man who had no intention of shooting them.

That's murder, isn't it?

'Wait, are you sure about this?' I ask Cole, not knowing what to believe any more.

'Yes, why would I lie?' he cries.

'I don't know. To get back at your parents for lying to you.'

'No, I'm not. I'm telling the truth. They wanted me to keep quiet and go along with their story but I'm not doing it. It's not fair.'

I can tell that Cole is being honest with me because there's a difference in the way he speaks compared to when Ryan tells me something. It feels genuine with Cole, whereas with my husband I'm starting to see that everything that comes out of his mouth is just designed to serve his best interests and no one else's.

'You're saying Kim killed Lewis and now her and Ryan are trying to cover it up?'

'Yes.'

I think about this for a moment then, but it quickly becomes clear there's only one thing we can do in the circumstances.

'Wait here. I'm going to get Emily.'

'Why?'

'Because we're leaving.'

'Now?'

'Yes, right now!'

It's perhaps what we should have done a long time ago, but now I've heard what Cole has to say there is no doubt in my mind. The three of us need to get as far away from Ryan and Kim as possible before they get back here and before they can do anything else to keep their secret quiet.

'Time to go,' I tell Emily, ushering her off the bed, and she's barely had a chance to close her book before I'm shepherding her out the door.

'Where are we going?' she asks, her little legs struggling to keep up with the pace I'm setting now.

'We're going home.'

'Is the car fixed?'

'Yes, but we're not taking the car.'

'Then how will we get home?'

'We're going to walk.'

'What?'

I don't actually mean we're going to walk all the way home, but we're certainly going to start our journey that way. On foot will be the quickest way we can get away from here before Ryan or Kim come back and ask us what we're doing.

Emily and I arrive at the front door of the cabin to see that Cole is already waiting for us.

'Should we take our things?' he asks me, looking at the suitcases I'd already packed and placed by the doors earlier.

'No, it'll only slow us down. We can get our stuff later.'

I make sure Emily is suitably attired for our trip into the forest as well as grabbing a couple of bottles of water before I open the door, leading Cole and my daughter outside.

A nervous glance at the treeline tells me that Ryan isn't back yet, nor is there any sign of Kim's car coming back down the track towards us.

'Okay, let's go,' I say, pointing to the direction I intend for us to travel in. It's a different route to the way I know both Kim and Ryan have gone, but that's only so we don't bump into them when they come back in the opposite direction. But we'll still be heading vaguely the way we need to go to get back to the main road, just taking the more scenic and discreet route.

'Why aren't we waiting for Daddy?' Emily asks as our feet crunch over the wet leaves and twigs.

'He's going to meet us there,' I say, hating that I have to lie, but in the circumstances it's a necessary one to keep my daughter moving.

Then it's Cole's turn to fire a question at me, but unlike with Emily I'm brutally honest with answering him.

'What's the plan when we get to the main road?' he asks.

'We call the police,' I say, not hesitating for a second. 'And then we tell them the truth.'

THIRTY-TWO

KIM

I hit both my hands against the steering wheel, briefly losing control of my emotions, and not for the first time since this car journey began I'm furious with myself. Angry. Disappointed. And worst of all, *guilty*.

I'm driving down the narrow track towards the main road, and when I get there I'm going to have to call the police and report my husband missing. That's the plan and it needs to be done. Until the police are involved then this can't be over. They need to come out here, find Lewis's body, ask a few questions and then, hopefully, call it a suicide and leave it at that.

That's what I want to happen.

But it doesn't mean that making it happen is going to be easy.

I'm doing my best to maintain a consistent, steady pace as I drive, my foot tentative on the accelerator because the mechanic told me to take it easy with the car during the initial stages after its battery had been brought back to life. It's a constant battle between doing that and wanting to put my foot down so I get to my destination quicker. The sooner I get to the main road and get a phone signal, the sooner I can get the call out of the way.

I've been trying to prepare myself for that call as I go, running through exactly what I'm going to say and trying to pre-empt some of the questions that are inevitably going to come back at me down the line. Questions like: how long has your husband been missing? Has this ever happened before? Do you think he might be hurt? What was his state of mind when he left? And possibly: are you telling me the truth?

I will have to be convincing and leave no room for doubt because doubt will only lead to more questions and that increases the odds that the police find out that I shot my husband.

Why did I pull the trigger? If it comes to it, I'll claim self-defence, but Ryan and I know that wasn't the case. Lewis had lowered his weapon. He wasn't going to shoot. The danger should have been over. But I fired anyway and, in doing so, I've created an even bigger problem than the one I had before.

Before pulling the trigger, all I had to deal with was knowing my husband and my son had discovered my lie. That was bad enough, but a dead body takes it to another level. It was my desperation to avoid some of the consequences from that first problem that caused me to shoot. I know, deep down, that in the moment when I held the gun in my hands and aimed it at Lewis, I saw a way to avoid so many difficult conversations. If Lewis lived then I would have to look him in the eye and explain to him how I have managed to go fifteen years allowing him to think of Cole as his own. Such an unbearable, soul-destroying conversation seemed like my idea of hell, and with the weapon in my hand I saw a way to avoid it.

Shoot and Lewis can't hate me, divorce me or do anything else to me that I deserve.

I guess I took the coward's way out. I neglected the long-term for a little short-term respite, and worst of all I thought I could get away with it. I still do, which makes me sick, but what other choice do I have? I can't go to prison, and I can't leave Cole. He's all I've got now.

Literally.

As I keep driving, I hit the wheel again, but this time it is because of sheer bad luck. Unashamedly, in the seconds before I killed Lewis, I thought about some of the things that might happen if he died and one of them was that his income from his thriving business would go to me. I was never with him just for his money, but at least I wouldn't have to worry about finances again when he was gone. But then Ryan went and told me that Lewis had confessed to him that his business was failing, and now I have no idea what money might be coming my way from my late husband. Anything? Nothing? Am I now liable for any debts my partner incurred while alive?

It's so overwhelming, and all that coupled with potentially having Cole hate me and never want to see me again leaves me feeling like I don't have any help in this world.

Apart from Ryan. He's been helping me so far, though I'm not sure why. I guess he's protecting me for Cole. He knows it's important the teenager has both his parents around. I doubt it's because he still harbours some feelings towards me. Even if he does, I can't even think about relationships right now.

As the end of the track suddenly comes into sight, my thoughts return quickly to the boys in blue.

I slow down as I approach the main road but not because I'm worried about any passing traffic. It's simply to delay the inevitable. Once on the road, I park by the side and reach for my mobile phone, to check the bars in the top right-hand corner. Unlike back at the cabin, I now have one. It might be enough to make a call but probably not, so I keep on driving until the signal strengthens.

As the tyres roll across the tarmac, I think about how, soon, this road will be filled with the tyres of all the emergency service vehicles coming to investigate the body in the woods. Police to cordon off the scene. Paramedics to inspect the body and take it away. Maybe some detective to start snooping around, sniffing for clues, hoping to uncover the truth, however grim it might be.

One thing is for sure.

This quiet place will soon be a lot busier.

I keep driving until I have three bars of signal on my phone and then I pull over before making the dreaded call.

Nine.

Nine.

Nine.

My hand is shaking as I hold my phone to my ear, and though the call connects quickly, it takes me a little longer to start speaking.

'My husband is missing.'

I eventually get the words out and the questions can begin. What's my name? What's my husband's name? Where are we? When did I last see him? When was he due back?

I'm told that normally a person isn't considered missing for seventy-two hours, but considering the remote region I'm calling from the dispatcher considers it wise to send for help in the form of mountain rescue.

'I don't think he's gone up a mountain,' I say, envisioning helicopters swarming the area.

'No, but he might have come into some difficulty in the terrain and the quickest way for us to determine that will be to have the rescue team come out.'

'Okay, I just want him found. I'm worried about him,' I say, aware how important it is that I seem anxious but not yet accepting that something bad has already happened.

I give the address of our holiday house and explain that I'm currently parked on the main road, but my son is back at the cabin, along with another family we came here with.

'Okay, I suggest you go back to the cabin and wait there for them. Help will be with you shortly.'

'Should I not wait here?'

'You can do, but it might take a while for them to get out to you. You may be more comfortable at home.'

I'm not sure which I prefer, sitting here in this car by myself or going back to that cabin and seeing other people.

'Your husband might return so it would be good if you were there when he did, so you would know to call us again.'

That makes sense so I tell the operator that I'll drive back to the holiday house now and then we end the call.

I throw my phone down on the seat beside me as if I can't bear to touch the device any longer now that I've just used it to begin the lie. That's it, it's in motion now. There's no going back. I have to stick to my story and not change anything.

Just like everyone else up here in this godforsaken place.

I turn the car around and get back on the track that leads to the cabin, thinking as I go about the first time that I came up here and how differently I felt then. I was so excited about owning a little piece of this landscape, but now I can't wait to see the back of this place because this is where my whole life fell apart.

I'm barely going more than 5 mph as I move down the track, every second taking me nearer to people who I either don't want to see or who don't want to see me. But it makes sense for me to be back at the cabin to wait for Lewis, so I force myself to keep going and when my holiday house comes into view, I wonder if Ryan will be back yet from his mission. Depending on how long it took him to find Lewis and switch the guns, he could be, but if not it will just be Nicola, Cole and Emily in there and that will be very awkward.

Then I see Ryan burst out of the front door and come running down the steps towards my car, and as I hit the brakes, I see he looks incredibly flustered.

I lower my window and poke my head out as he gets closer.

'What is it?' I ask him, afraid for what might have happened next. Has Cole hurt himself? Has Nicola asked more difficult questions? Or could Ryan not find the body and hasn't been able to hide the second gun?

It turns out none of those things has happened. *Something even worse has.*

'They've gone!' Ryan cries, his eyes wide and afraid.

'What?'

'There's nobody in there! They've left!'

'What do you mean they've left?'

I look at the empty cabin behind him, but seeing no movement in there I have to believe him.

'I got back five minutes ago, but there's no one in there,' Ryan tells me. 'I checked every room and ran around the whole cabin. Wherever they are, they're not here!'

'Well, they must be on foot. They can't have got far,' I say, but that doesn't seem to calm his nerves, and it's only when I ask him why Nicola might have chosen to leave unexpectedly with Cole and Emily that he shows me something terrible.

'I found this on the kitchen counter,' he says, handing me a piece of paper, and when I turn it over I see what is scribbled on the other side of it. It's a word that makes it clear exactly why Nicola has left, as well as providing an insight into what she might be planning to do if we don't catch up to her before she talks to the police.

One word.

Five letters.

Liars.

THIRTY-THREE

NICOLA

'Keep a hold of my hand,' I say to Emily as we move on through the forest, my fear of her letting go and then getting herself lost almost as strong as the fear that I might see Ryan coming through the trees at any moment.

Emily does as she is told, clearly understanding that something serious is going on here and there's no time for games, while Cole walks on the other side of me, saying very little but moving quickly, showing he is still happy to comply with my plan to get out of here and talk to the police.

While encountering Ryan and having him ask us where we are going is a concern, at least we don't have to worry about Kim because we're still well clear of the track, and it is a good job we are because we heard the sound of a car passing by not so long ago, and I assume that was her returning to the cabin. If so then that means she has already made the initial call to the police in which she has reported Lewis missing, which makes the phone call I am planning on making even more imperative. It also means she is probably back at the cabin by now and will have realised that we've gone. Once she knows that, she'll be straight back out to look for us to find out where we might be going. But if either Kim or Ryan are in any doubt as to why the three of us are on the move now then I will have removed it with the note I left behind for them to find.

Perhaps it would have been wiser not to write it, but I couldn't resist. I wanted both of them to know that they had been caught out and I wasn't as gullible as they thought. Calling them both liars, a title each of them richly deserves, was meant to send them into a panic when they read it, and if they're panicking, that means they won't be thinking straight. If they're not thinking straight, they will most likely take longer to find us than if they were calm and rational, and with a bit of luck their desperation will cause them to argue with each other and lose the only ally that each of them has now.

I'm also aware that staying off the main track and traipsing through the dense trees is slowing our progress down, not to mention increasing the chances of us getting lost out here. What if they find us before we can call for help? And what would they do to us if they think we are a threat?

I console myself by doubting Ryan or Kim would hurt Emily or Cole. No matter how desperate they might be, neither of them would want to harm their own flesh and blood. But what about me? Am I fair game?

Hopefully, I won't have to find out.

It seems I'm not the only one worrying because Cole asks me what might happen if they catch up to us, reminding me that they have the gun, not that I needed such a reminder.

'We'll be fine,' I reply, not wanting either of us to dwell on the firearms our pursuers might possess. 'They might not even be trying to find us,' I add, although that is rather hopeful even for me.

'Of course they will,' Cole tells me. 'Have you seen what they're like now? They'll do anything to get what they want.'

'What is he talking about?' Emily asks, complicating our

conversation somewhat, although now I know that her presence here isn't going to stop Cole talking about such things.

'It's okay, darling,' I say, giving Emily's hand a squeeze before letting go of it and asking her if she would like to go ahead of us.

'See if you can find our way through,' I tell her. 'But stay close. Don't run off and get too far ahead.'

Emily likes the idea of being the leader, so she breaks away from us and does her best job of showing the way, not that she knows it any better than I do. I'm OK with that as long as I can keep my eyes on her, and with her now out of earshot it does mean one thing.

I can talk to Cole much more easily.

'I understand you're worried. But you have to be careful what you say around Emily. She doesn't know what's going on yet and she's too young to understand.'

'I know and I'm sorry. I'm just worried.'

'Me too. But we'll be okay.'

'I'm worried about you.'

I pause for a moment when Cole says that because it's caught me by surprise. He's worried about me?

'I know they won't hurt me or Emily,' he explains. 'But I saw what they did to Dad. He just got shot. Now I'm worried they'll do the same to you.'

'Nobody else is getting shot,' I say, hoping he believes me and almost hoping I can believe it myself. 'We're going to make it to the road and the police will keep us safe.'

'Yeah, but only when they get here and when will that be?'

I have no answer for that one, so I carry on walking, increasing my speed when I see that Emily has gotten a little too far ahead of us.

We carry on for around half an hour and I'm just about thinking we're completely lost when Emily suddenly lets out an excited cry from ahead.

'I can see the road,' she says, pointing to something in the distance, and as Cole and I catch up to her we see she is right. There is tarmac through the trees and that means we should be able to get a phone signal soon. We just have to find the right spot on the road to get it.

Cole takes off running and despite me calling after him to slow down and be careful, he doesn't take heed and he's soon away from us. Emily wants to go almost as quickly as he just did, but I tell her to take her time and be careful so that she doesn't trip, and we make our way together.

By the time we get there, Cole already has his phone out and is searching for a signal, although it doesn't seem he has got one yet. I quickly check my phone, but I have the same amount of luck as the teenager, so we both keep moving down the road to try and improve our chances.

Every second we are out here in the open makes me nervous because I know Kim and Ryan could come along in the car and catch us before we've had chance to make the call, but with no other way of picking up a signal, it's a risk we have to take. And then just like that, we get lucky.

'Got it!' I cry, the bars on my phone screen telling me calls can be made now. I dare not move from the square of tarmac that I'm on in case I lose it again.

I waste no time in contacting the police and no sooner have they picked up than I tell them exactly what the problem is.

'We're in danger,' I say before giving my location and telling them to send help immediately. Things get tricky when they ask me for more details about the nature of the danger that I'm in because Emily is standing beside me, but one look at Cole and he gets the hint that he needs to move my daughter away, so he takes her to the other side of the road to look at some daffodils.

I tell the operator that a man has been shot and we're potentially at risk of being shot too, and while I'm assured that help is already on the way, I'm asked for further details of the threat.

But there's no time for that because a second later I freeze when I hear the sound of a car engine approaching.

Cole hears it too and looks down the road in the direction it's coming from.

'Hide!' I cry, gesturing for him to take Emily and get behind the nearest tree, and he does as I say as I run to join them.

I see Emily trip and fall as she is pulled off the road and onto the grassy embankment, but Cole yanks her back to her feet, and by the time I catch up with them, they're both crouching down behind a sturdy piece of oak.

'Be quiet,' I say to them both, putting a finger to my lips to illustrate my point.

The car is getting closer and as I wait for it to come into view, I'm praying that it's a different make and model to the vehicle we have left behind.

But it's not. It's Kim's car.

They're here.

They've caught us.

THIRTY-FOUR

NICOLA

I keep my finger to my lips as the car gets nearer, slowly moving down the road while the heads of the two occupants inside it look from side to side. I can see Kim behind the wheel and Ryan sitting beside her and both of them are looking for us, as they well might.

But will they find us, or is this hiding place going to be enough to keep us safe?

Seeing the two of them together as if they're working as a team makes me feel hollow inside, like it's almost as much of a betrayal as what they did in the past. It's because I know Ryan should be by my side, not hers, and I should be with him instead of feeling like I have to run from him.

'It's Daddy!' Emily suddenly cries and before either Cole or I can stop her, she darts out into the road.

'Emily, no!' I call, reaching out for her arm to try and pull her back as the car gets closer.

But then it hits the brakes and despite dragging Emily back, I know it's too late. They've just seen us.

What are they going to do now?

'I don't understand why we're hiding,' Emily whines after I scold her for leaving our hiding place, and as much as I wish my daughter hadn't just revealed our position, I know much of the blame for her doing so lies with me because I didn't explain to her why we had to stay away from Ryan. As far as she is concerned, she's just seen her daddy and wants to go to him, like any young girl would.

I should have told her the truth.

Daddy might be dangerous.

'We need to go,' Cole says and it's clear he'd rather run back into the forest than stay here and let Kim or Ryan ask him why we were trying to get away. In the split second I have to make a decision, I consider all our options. The police have been called so we could run and try and hide until they get here, although we'll still be chased and there's no guarantee we'll be able to avoid Kim and Ryan for all that time. If we do run, it will only confirm to the pair that we are against them and that increases the chances they will do something drastic. If we don't run, they will catch us, but they won't know the police are coming and maybe I could just say we left because we were anxious in the cabin and needed some fresh air. We've come a long way from the holiday house, far further than what could be considered a short walk, but they don't have to know we were running from them.

And then I remember the note I left behind, the one in which I called them both liars. I'm not sure how I could spin that into something positive, and as Kim and Ryan get out of the car and call to us I make my decision.

Cole is right.

We should run again.

'Go!' I say, pointing to the trees, and Cole is already off, sprinting as fast as he can. But Emily is dawdling, looking back at her dad instead of looking where we are going, and I can't keep up. There's no way I'll leave her behind, so I keep pulling her, but she keeps calling for her dad and giving away our position.

'Come on! We have to go!' I try and I pull Emily with me, just getting to the point where I think she might be complying. But it doesn't matter if she is because what I hear next makes both of us freeze, as well as Cole ahead of us.

'Stop or I'll shoot!'

Ryan's command chills me to the bone. He wouldn't dare, would he? But with Emily to protect, I'm too afraid to test him, so we turn back around to face him. When he sees me, he notes the phone in my hand.

'What have you done?' he asks me, clearly afraid that I might have called the police before they got here and contradicted what Kim told them.

'Nothing,' I lie, hoping he'll buy it.

'Who have you called?'

'Nobody!'

'Now who's the liar?'

'I mean it. I was going to call the police, but you turned up before I got a signal.'

I hold my breath while I wait to see if Ryan believes me.

'Put the phone down,' he says calmly.

'Why?'

'Just do it.'

I look at Emily and then Cole, as if to let them know that I don't have much choice, before I place the phone on the ground between myself and Ryan.

Kim is standing just beside him, and she hasn't spoken yet. But the gun in my husband's hand is doing enough talking for everyone.

'Daddy, why have you got a gun?' Emily asks, her innocent little voice sounding ridiculous in such a tense situation.

'It's okay, darling. It's safe. I just need to talk to Mummy.'

'Just leave us alone,' Cole interjects, his voice much harsher than my daughter's.

'Why were you trying to call the police?' Ryan asks me.

'I don't know.'

'What do you mean you don't know?'

'I was scared.'

'Of what?'

I can hardly say of the two people standing in front of me now, so I need something else.

'We just want to go home. All three of us.'

'And we will go home. But we had a plan, and you should have stuck to it.'

'I know and I'm sorry. But it's okay, right?'

I'm trying to find something in Ryan's expression that reminds me of the man I once thought he was. But there's nothing there. He looks so different now. So cold.

'You left us a note in the cabin,' he says, the gun still by his side. 'What did it mean?'

'Nothing.'

'You called us liars.'

'Did I?'

I'm stalling as best I can, but I know it's still going to be a while before the police get here and there's only so much I can do.

'Cole, what did you say?' Kim asks her son, finally speaking.

'Nothing,' he mumbles back, but she's not buying it and keeps asking him.

Cole says nothing, which is probably for the best, and it gives me a chance to try and deescalate the situation.

'Look, Emily is scared. How about we all just get in the car and go back to the cabin?'

'Not until you tell us why you left it in the first place,' Ryan snaps back.

'Why do you think?' I reply just as quickly, putting the onus on him to talk his way out of his mess.

'I have no idea.'

'I think you do.'

The distance between us might not have changed physically, but I can feel it growing wider in so many other ways as we stand here and stare at each other by the side of this road.

'Because I told the truth,' Cole suddenly says, speaking much more clearly than the last time he opened his mouth. 'I told Nicola what you did. Both of you. You killed Dad.'

'What?'

Emily looks at me, extremely confused and afraid. 'Is Lewis hurt?'

I don't know what to say to that, but Ryan and Kim are only bothered about what Cole just said.

'It was self-defence,' Kim tries lamely, but Cole scoffs.

'No, it wasn't. Dad lowered his gun. But you still shot him anyway. And now you're trying to cover it up by making it look like he killed himself.'

I see the flicker of emotion on Ryan's face when Cole calls Lewis his dad, and I wonder if Cole will ever truly recognise the man standing in front of him as his real father. Acting like this won't help matters, that's for sure.

'I just want you to tell the truth,' Cole begs. 'Both of you. For the first time in my life, be honest. Please!'

Cole's passionate plea is a heart-breaking one, not least because it's so honest. Kim and Ryan have lied to him since he was born and they're still doing it to this day.

Until now, it seems.

'You're right,' Kim says ruefully. 'We have lied to you and we're sorry. Both of us. We never meant to hurt you. Any of you. Things just got out of hand, but we've only ever wanted to protect you.'

'How is killing Dad protecting me?' Cole quite rightly asks.

'It was the heat of the moment. I panicked,' Kim admits, her voice and expression full of sorrow.

'He wasn't going to hurt you.'

'I know that now.'

I'm surprised that Kim is admitting it, but maybe there is still a good person in there somewhere, buried beneath all the lies. But what about Ryan?

'We're just trying to keep our families together, that's all,' he says. 'That's why we need to tell the police that Lewis killed himself. It's the best way to ensure no one goes to prison and we all stay together.'

'Who's going to prison?' Emily asks.

'Nobody, darling,' Ryan says before he smiles at me, as if that can make up for everything that has gone before. 'Right, Nic?'

I know that I will disappoint somebody, whatever answer I give. It might be Cole, or it might be Ryan, but there's only one of them with a gun so in the end it's an easy choice.

'Right,' I say quietly.

Ryan and Kim relax instantly once they know I'm back on side and they quickly start making a plan for how to manage this situation further.

'Let's get back to the cabin and wait for the police to turn up,' Ryan says. 'When they do, we'll stick to our original story, and everything will be fine. We'll be home by the end of the day, all right?'

'But—'

'That sounds good to me,' I say, cutting off Cole before he can protest again.

'Come on, let's go,' Ryan says, ushering us to the car, and I tell Emily to follow him, only stopping to pick my phone off the ground before joining her at the vehicle.

'I can't believe you're doing this,' Cole says to me as he lingers behind me.

'Just get in the car,' I tell him, praying he'll just follow. 'Everything will be okay, I promise.'

While he has clearly lost all respect for the other adults here, there must still be some for me because Cole does as I say. Once the three of us are on the back seat, Ryan gets behind the wheel and Kim sits beside him before we set off back towards the cabin.

It's a quiet, tense ride down the track, one that is missing all the chatter, humour and anticipation of the last time we were all in a car together, and by the time the holiday house comes into view again, I'm glad the journey is at an end.

Kim takes the gun as we go inside, to put it back in the box it came here in, while Ryan nervously checks his watch, anxious about the arrival of the police and the search team for Lewis. I do the only thing I can think of to keep Emily and Cole happy, which is to take out some snacks and make them a drink and it's a relief to see my daughter tucking in, although Cole just sits with his arms crossed in front of his chest and glares at the wall.

Kim and Ryan both apologise to us all again while we sit and wait for somebody to get here, but other than that the conversation is at a minimum, until we hear the sound of tyres on the track outside.

Ryan rushes to the window before saying 'they're here', and I've never felt so relieved in my life to see a police officer as I do when I see the uniform get out of the car. I'm even more relieved when they reach the cabin door, because despite Kim telling them she is worried about her husband and Ryan advising them on which direction he left in, the only thing the officers are interested in doing is putting handcuffs on.

Ryan and Kim look as shocked as each other as their hands are drawn behind their backs and their rights are read out to them. Emily is scared and Cole is confused, but I'm not because I'm the only one who had some idea this might happen.

I'm the only one who knew that I never ended my phone

call to the police earlier when Ryan and Kim caught up to us by the side of the road.

I'm the only one who knew the police were listening in the whole time.

EPILOGUE
NICOLA

As I gaze out of my living room window with a cup of tea in hand, I don't see any pine forests, snow-capped mountains or still blue lochs. But that's perfectly fine by me.

It's been six months since I was in Scotland and I can't say I've missed the place, although I know that has far more to do with what happened there than the scenery. Half a year is a long time to process emotions but not such a long time in the British legal system, because despite Kim being arrested and charged with murder, and Ryan himself charged with conspiracy to prevent the course of justice as well as the more serious charge of threatening his wife and daughter with a weapon, neither of them have gone to trial yet. But their lawyers think they can get the charges knocked down or at least have their final punishments severely reduced, mainly thanks to the fact that Lewis did have a gun himself when he was shot, so they can argue they felt threatened and pressured into acting the way they did. But, despite still technically being married to Ryan, he's not my concern any more. We're separated now and our divorce is inevitable, and it was inevitable the moment he threatened me and my daughter with a gun.

I have no idea if he would have shot at us if we had carried on running away from that road and I wasn't willing to put him to the test. But the fact it was even an option told me that I could never love him like I once had. Given enough time, perhaps I could forgive a one-night stand and maybe even the lies that followed regarding Cole.

But I could not forgive him risking Emily's life.

The house is quiet, my daughter currently at a friend's place and back to doing what a girl her age should be doing, which is mainly having fun and not worrying about things. She's had plenty of questions for me since what happened, and I know she'll only have more as she gets older, but, for now, she seems settled enough and that is all I care about.

Maybe that's not strictly true however, because there is someone else that I care about at the moment. It's Cole, the poor teenager who also had his life turned upside down after that fateful weekend away. He's been staying with Kim's parents since all the trouble and doing his best to try and concentrate on schoolwork. Quite how he's managing to focus on such a thing at this time is beyond me, but I have been very impressed by the reports from his grandparents when I have checked in on him. I've been checking regularly since we got back from Scotland, wanting to know that Cole is okay and even reaching out to him myself a few times to let him know that I am always here for him, if he needs any support. There was even a time when I considered inviting him to stay with me permanently, before I knew his grandparents could have him, wanting to provide him with a safe and settled home to counterbalance all the upheaval that was going on in other parts of his life. It was mainly out of the goodness of my heart that I was prepared to make such a gesture, but I have to admit there was also a part of me that felt having Cole here to look after would have been getting back at Kim and Ryan slightly, the two people who should have always been looking out for him, but the two people who had let him down so badly. That might be a little spiteful, but they did hunt us down in a forest and threaten us with a gun, so how much is too much when it comes to those two?

I've done my best to keep myself busy over these last six months, trying to find some contentment in my relatively simple life, particularly when compared to the life of Kim, my former best friend who once seemed to have it all but now has nothing. Whereas I have been going to work, paying my modest bills and maintaining my humble home, I know that she has been trying to live life without Lewis while the court case looms over her. With her income gone and the fallout of Lewis's failing business to unravel, life will certainly be very different for Kim even if she manages to avoid prison. Gone will be the big house, fast car and lavish holidays. Speaking of holidays, what became of the holiday house in the Highlands, the one that was once the envy of all those who were taken there by its owners? The last I heard, it was being sold and the proceeds were due to pay off the many tax bills that Lewis's business had incurred but neglected while the owner was alive. I'm not sure if a buyer has been found for it yet, but whoever eventually ends up with the keys will most likely never know the full extent of the drama that occurred both under its roof and within the surrounding area.

The bombshell in the hot tub. The gunfire in the forest. And the swarm of police officers who descended on the cabin and took away the guilty parties. Things like that have no place in an estate agent's spiel, so I guess the new buyers will always be in the dark about it all. Unlike those who were there when it all happened.

We'll never forget that time.

I leave my vantage point by the window and head into the kitchen to make myself another cup of tea, careful not to trip over several of Emily's items that litter the floor as they tend to do in this house. I'm always tidying up after her, but I guess that's just one of my many jobs while she's under this roof, until she grows up, gets her own place and learns to fend for herself. But that's okay because I'll do anything for her, just like I guess Kim and Ryan would do anything for Cole.

They obviously felt that keeping their secret about how he was conceived was the best thing for him, although they had their own selfish reasons, like preserving their respective relationships. I don't know if Cole will ever be able to forgive them for the lies that they told him, but I know they are both extremely anxious to find out. I wouldn't blame Cole if he never wanted to see either of them again though and the fact such a thing has been left up to chance terrifies me. I can't imagine waiting and wishing that my child would still want to be a part of my life and, thankfully, I'll never have to go through such a thing.

I won't because unlike Kim and Ryan I'll ensure the secret I have will never come out.

As I wait for the kettle to boil, I stare at a photo of Emily that I keep on a magnet on the fridge. It's of her as a little baby, just one month old and looking extremely cute in a pink dress with matching bonnet. She was such a sweet, innocent girl and still is mostly, but the same cannot be said for her mother.

The kettle clicks to let me know that it has boiled and the hot water is ready to be poured into my mug with the teabag, but I don't reach for it, instead finding myself lost in one of the daydreams that envelopes me on occasion and drags me back twelve years to the night I made a dreadful mistake of my own.

The night Ryan and I argued, each of us tired, frustrated and afraid after yet another month of me failing to conceive. The same night I stormed out of the house because I needed some time to myself only to end up in a bar in town drinking wine all alone. That very night a kind man came to keep me company and told me all the things I hadn't heard from my own husband in a while, like how I was beautiful and how I should smile more often because I lit up a room when I did.

That was the night I slept with someone else and, as far as I can tell, it was the same night I got pregnant with Emily. Or maybe it wasn't. Maybe Emily is Ryan's and that one-night stand was not as terrible as it might have been. The truth is *I don't know*. Ryan might be Emily's father, or it could be that other guy, the guy whose name I forgot because I was so drunk and I never saw him again after leaving his place once we had done the drunken deed.

I was too scared to get a paternity test, choosing to believe that the baby growing inside me was my husband's and no one else's. But having kept it a secret for this long, that's the way I'll keep it until I die. I never want to know the truth and, if I don't know, Ryan and Emily can never know either.

The steam is rising out of the kettle and the water still needs to be used, but I've suddenly lost my desire for a cup of tea and a biscuit. This tends to happen when I momentarily think back to what may or may not be in regards to my daughter.

So why can't I forgive Ryan for cheating if I'm guilty of doing the same thing? I guess the big difference is I found out about his mistake while he has never found out about mine, nor will he. I tell myself that I might have forgiven him in time if only he didn't have that gun, but maybe I'm secretly glad he did threaten me because that makes me justify not forgiving him even more.

The thought of Emily finding out that Ryan might not be her dad and that I knew about it scares me to death because then she'll be no different to Cole. But she doesn't know and that's why she still loves me wholeheartedly, like a daughter should love her mother, and that's a love I can't afford to lose.

I can handle losing everything else.

But not that.

I eventually manage to banish the terrible thoughts and

consign them back to whatever box I keep them in in my mind until it pops open again unexpectedly, so I finish making my tea and return to the sofa. When I get there, I notice it's raining outside now, even though the forecast said it was supposed to be nice. Typical British weather, I guess. Such a thing usually makes me long for a holiday and it would be easy to lose myself in a fantasy involving sun, sea and sand, but I don't entertain those thoughts any more than I care to entertain the thoughts about my past mistake. I don't entertain them because I know a holiday is not always the answer to life's problems. If anything, a holiday can often serve to be the start of them.

That holiday home has a lot to answer for.

I guess I'll have to be careful where I go in future.

And who I go with.

A LETTER FROM DANIEL

Dear reader,

I want to say a huge thank you for choosing to read *The Holiday Home*. If you did enjoy it and would like to keep up to date with all my latest releases, please sign up at the following link. Your email address will never be shared and you can unsubscribe at any time.

www.bookouture.com/daniel-hurst

I hope you loved *The Holiday Home* and, if you did, I would be very grateful if you could write an honest review. I'd love to hear what you think, and it makes such a difference in helping new readers to discover my books for the first time.

I love hearing from my readers, and you can get in touch with me directly at my email address daniel@danielhurstbooks.-com. I reply to every message! You can also visit my website where you can download a free psychological thriller called *Just One Second*.

Thank you,

Daniel

KEEP IN TOUCH WITH DANIEL

www.danielhurstbooks.com

 facebook.com/danielhurstbooks
instagram.com/danielhurstbooks